A Jacana book

Kitchen Casualties

Willemien de Villiers

First published in 2003 by **Jacana**
5 St Peter Road
Bellevue
2198
South Africa

2003 © Willemien de Villiers

ISBN 1-919931-12-0

Cover design by **Disturbance**
disturb@mweb.co.za

Printed by **Formeset Printers**

See a complete list of Jacana titles at www.jacana.co.za

Acknowledgments

My heartfelt thanks to tenacious fairy godmother, Karin Cronjé, and Thérèse Bartman, for her friendship and her poems. For enthusiastic dedication and insight I thank my editor Lynda Gilfillan, as well as Lynda Harvey and Maggie Davey. Special thanks to Anne Schuster – where it all started – my gratitude and thanks for her encouragement and support.

This is a work of fiction and all characters are imaginary.

For my daughters, Klara and Ella

Isabel

The female Vapourer moth, my husband once told me, is wingless, and all she ever does is wait. This is a fact.

"She emerges from her cocoon, and immediately produces a scent that a male can smell five kilometres away." Fact.

"You'll find these moths on hazel and hawthorn trees." Another fact.

"What happens after mating?" I asked.

"She lays hundreds of eggs, on top of her own discarded cocoon. And then she dies. Having no wings, she has no choice."

"She can't escape her destiny and fly away?"

Jonathan shook his head and brought me a spirally twisted seedpod from the desk in his study. I was standing on the balcony next to our bedroom, watching the sun set into the saddle of the Noordhoek mountains. The swarm of yellow-clad experts, turning the area opposite our home into a functioning wetland system, were getting into their Nissan bakkies and driving away.

"This is an Umbrella thorn seedpod. Very nutritious for elephants, real bushveld food. Bagworm moths live in these trees, and they have a much more exotic, harem-style existence than the Vapourer Moth." He placed the green seed in my hand.

Jonathan leaned his elbows next to mine on the railing of the balcony and together we looked down at the emerging wetland.

For months, men in bright yellow overalls, rain gear for the anticipated wet stormy days, have been reshaping the previously "alien-infested area" as it was described in the local newspaper. First they cleared away the illegal squatters, then the

9

illegal alien vegetation; Port Jackson willow, brought over from Australia to stabilise our dunes. A clump of wattle still stood in the centre of a large cleared area, waiting to be removed.

"Poor Jackson," I named it as a child, feeling sorry for the unwanted plant. He pointed at it, saying, "One species of Bagworm moth thrives in that, the wattle over there."

"You know everything," I smiled, turning to go inside.

Yellow excavators scooped up loads of earth, swivelling around and dumping it somewhere else. Reshaping and tunnelling so that the river can flow once more. This is being done in anticipation of the next 40-year flood, a rare flash of foresight not often found in a swollen bureaucracy.

"Tell me more about the Bagworm moths," I asked, following Jonathan to the kitchen. "What is it that makes them so special?"

"They weave silky bags from waste fragments to lay their eggs in." Pouring two glasses of wine, he passed one to me. "These bags are sometimes communal."

People love telling me things. Feeding me facts, like my mother used to do, and still does.

"And the female moths are not only wingless, like the Vapourer, but also without mouth-parts or feelers. After mating, and laying the eggs, they die inside their silk-lined bag."

"Just like that? End of moth?"

Jonathan popped a potato chip into his mouth, nodding.

"Yip, just like that."

He wasn't telling me about these moths to convey some hidden message or agenda. It was just a bit of information that was passed along, like peas and gravy during supper. Along with all the other crumbs of information, strewn on the path of our life together. Breadcrumbs to find the way home.

Gloria

It is six o'clock in the morning and the sun is just beginning to draw a line of light where the two curtains meet. Outside her window she hears waves crashing against the rocks.

Gloria kicks at the heavy eiderdown. Her mother quilted it in the months before Gloria's birth almost a century ago and it will not last to keep another generation warm. The patterned flowers have faded to a soft-focus blur of greens and pinks, and small cream-coloured tufts of stuffing are escaping through moth holes.

Her back is turned to her husband's snores, a chorus of spittle, as she breaststrokes back to a dream filled with watery ancestors. In this dream she taps Frankie on his shoulder with her finger. She wants to tell him that she is pregnant with their child.

"Why can't you just be Frank," she mumbles, "Why Frankie, like Johnny, Tommy . . . such silly names . . . "

The sound of Frankie's snoring returns, and she wakes up, but doesn't open her eyes.

She is resentful of his sleep and sits up in the bed, thumps her pillow. Her husband's name echoes in the air. She sighs loudly. If she can't sleep, neither will he. She keeps her eyes closed, anticipating blindness, for she is nearing her century birthday.

A Bible lies on the floor next to her bed. They have taken all the other tranquillisers away, and left her only this one. She leans over to place her bookmark between two random pages, for later, when she opens her eyes to read her own private message from God. As she leans down she overbalances and tumbles from the bed, pulling the quilt with her.

Sitting up, she moves back onto her bottom until she is resting against the side of the bed. This is the rescue position that her daughter knows well, always arriving in time to save her mother. From habit, Gloria feels for the scattered pills on the pine floorboards, but finds none.

Waking up in hospital after another unsuccessful suicide attempt, she always saw Ruth and Dr Roberts looking down at her like disapproving parents. They never understood that she meant her death to be a last gift to her daughter.

"Oh Mother, what am I to do with you?" Ruth would say, her mouth an upside-down horseshoe with all the good luck running out.

With the Bible in her left hand Gloria shuffles blindly to the bathroom, lifting Frankie's old shirt as she eases herself onto the toilet seat. She rests the Bible on her thighs and presses with her left and right index fingers onto each cheekbone, hard, until it hurts. The bright line of light between the curtains dances behind her closed eyelids.

"*Dis sommer 'n klomp stront,*" she mumbles in her dead mother's tongue. Afrikaans words escape early in the mornings, before she is properly awake.

"A lot of nonsense," she repeats, "All this fuss."

Isabel

A small moth with a sturdy body shaped like a wingnut sits on the green shade of my reading lamp. Light from the lamp illuminates a framed black and white photograph of my daughter, hanging on the wall next to my bed. When I look at it I see her love for Timo, who took this photograph. It is into his eyes that she is smiling, not mine.

By the time Morgan discovered her love of Scotland, her heart already belonged to someone else. She had met Timo Carelse at the Serendipity Gallery in Cape Town, where final year design students from the Cape Technikon were exhibiting photography work.

Instead of the wide-angled views of hardship in the Cape Flats suburbs where he grew up, Timo photographed the open hands of a hundred residents, palms facing up. By using a close-up lens, and over-exposing the film, the hands turned into landscapes viewed from an aeroplane, showing lines criss-crossing; becoming thin cattle-tracks on bare ground. These images were juxtaposed with photographs of out-of-focus faces, arbitrarily framed and shot. His deliberate Boo-Boo-Bin pictures cut off mouths, eyes were lost, left only half a face showing.

"What do you make of this?" I asked Morgan when she took me to the exhibition.

"I don't know, at first I just enjoyed how they look, the feel of the hands, the softness of the faces, but the more I look, the more I get a sense of what he is trying to say."

"You mean alternating the two different images? Faces and hands?"

A young man entered the room and a patch of red bloomed onto Morgan's chest. I could see that she was falling in love with the artist, as well as the art.

He walked over, smiled at me, and touched her shoulder.

"You were at the opening last night," he said.

"And I made you your first sale," she replied.

"Which one?"

I moved away as she walked to a photograph of two large eyes, upturned towards something or someone, invisible to the viewer. Even though they were out of focus, or maybe because of it, the eyes looked startled, surprised.

"Why do you like this one?" he asked Morgan. His head tilted to one side as he listened to her answer, nodding every now and then, smiling.

The outside surface of my bedroom wall is covered with hundreds of yellow cocoons, spun by the small Wingnut moths. They are attracted by the large fig tree in the courtyard. Morgan used to pull the cocoons from the wall to show me the segmented grubs inside, visible through the thinly spun underside. Those veiled grubs reminded me of the glass-covered heads of dead birds in Morgan's bird cemetery.

After a short funeral service in which she told the deceased that they were "now free to fly forever," Morgan placed the small corpses inside a hollow in the ground and covered them up with soil, except for their heads, which remained visible under a clear piece of glass.

"I want to see what happens when you die," she explained, and kneeled next to these glass coffins after school to watch ants and worms clean the feathers and flesh from the bones.

*

Through the open window a waxing moon etches a narrow curve, like that of a boning knife, onto the pale morning sky.

I start to make my bed. When I woke up this morning Jonathan's side was empty, his pillow plumped up, head-hollow erased. His side of the bed neatly tucked in and smooth.

I strip it bare, removing the fitted bottom sheet, top sheet, two thin blankets, a heavy, embroidered green cover. I strip it down to the blue satin of our mattress. The layering of our bed used to fascinate my daughter, Morgan. Or rather, the amount of time I spent remaking it every day.

Jonathan and I fold the sheets outside on the bright green square of noonday sun. It is an act of intimacy, a slow dance we perform as we face each other, holding two corners each. The sheet forms a brilliant hammock, wide enough to hold thoughts, desires, memories.

His sunglasses reflect a small version of me as we fold corner to corner, shake and stretch. I hand him my open corners and walk back with the closed side. Then one more shake and fold.

We do not speak during our ritual of folding.

"All you need is a futon and a duvet," Morgan told me when she was still living under our roof.

"Timo and I just bought one, it doesn't need so much fussing," she added. I took them a set of pale stoneware mugs as a housewarming gift, and sat down on their folded futon couch. It reminded me of the *Such-and-Such* chair I invented when I was six years old. Whenever my mother told me that I was *such* a liar, the emphasis she put on that word made me lose myself in its sound. *Such*. Such a word! *Such* a liar! It became a hammock when I wrote it on paper in the looping forms of my first written words. I imagined curling up in the *u* and dangling one arm over the *c,* stroking the *s* with the other.

I told our neighbour's daughter, my best friend Sarie, that Ruth had made me a foam rubber chair, shaping the word *such*.

"Can I come and see it?" Sarie demanded, and naturally I asked my mother to turn my lie into a belated truth. Of course all she said was, "Isabel, you are *such* a liar!"

Arguing with Morgan, I often felt those same words form in my throat, felt my mother taking up residence there. I swallowed hard to get rid of her.

I pick up my watch lying on the bedside table, next to a pile of books about Scotland. A page of poetry falls to the floor, along with the seedpod Jonathan gave me last night, talking about moths.

bredie

dae lank al druis die reën
maar op die stoof is
lamsvleis losgestoom van been
is uie en tamatie, murg en knoffel
salig een

het ek maar 'n vers gemaak
wat na urelange prut
só geurig was;
die volheid van elke woord
losgekook
en opgeneem
herinnering aan jou is opgekerf
my mes is skerp so skerp.
Sal ek liefde hierby waag?

op dié aftreksel sit ek die deksel
en draai die plaat op laag.

I am translating the work of Afrikaans poet, Thérèse Bartman.

Whenever I hear of attempts to preserve Afrikaans, by those who believe it is a dying language, I am reminded of the rows of clear Consol Glass bottles that stand in my pantry, filled by my mother Ruth with preserved peaches, apricots and pears. When you preserve something all growth stops. Translating one language into another gives birth to something new. Translating poetry is attempting the impossible.

Bredie. The word carries with it the fragrant smell of nourishment; it could be a smell from my mother's kitchen. The dictionary will inform you that it means *stew.* But a *bredie* is not a stew. *Stew* is the sound of anger, of being "in a stew" over something or another. It suggests heat and escaped steam, not a slow blending and simmering.

So I continue my search, turning words over like stones, looking for scorpions or treasures underneath.

I prefer translating Afrikaans into English, rather than the other way round. I love the flow of English; the ease with which I can twist and plait and coil a sentence. English is a willow tree with evergreen sappy boughs and Afrikaans a *kokerboom* with poison arrows. I don't trust her with my heart, where my true voice lies. When I write my mother tongue the words constrict like a hangman's rope.

This poem tells of a pot of *bredie* on a stove, of tender lamb's meat steamed free from the bone, of onion and tomato and marrow *salig een.* In blissful union. Outside the kitchen that holds the stove, and the pot, there is the sound of rain. *Dae lank al druis die reën.*

Untranslatable onomatopoeic description.

It ponders, wistfully, the outcome of words left to simmer for hours, *die volheid van elke woord/losgekook/en opgeneem*. The full and fragrant meaning of each word as it falls free from the bones and sinews of language, absorbed as thoughts and feelings. Could that be what the poet is saying? I close my eyes and try to call up a feeling devoid of language, but all too soon words appear and interfere.

Into this *bredie* the poet adds the sharp spice of love. *Sal ek liefde hierby waag?* is the question she asks. Dare she add love?

She prepared the *bredie* with sharpened knives, cutting up the ingredients, and adding memories of a loved one into the simmering pot. Then replaced the lid and turned the heat to low.

op dié aftreksel sit ek die deksel
en draai die plaat op laag.

Translation deadlocks tie my tongue into a knot for weeks while I search for the right word or phrase. Weighing one against the other. Words appear and disappear with the same randomness as a forgotten dream. Sometimes the blink of an eye can make them appear.

Blink again, and they are gone.

I slide a piece of paper under the moth and lift it from the lampshade. Jonathan's moth stories tell the beginning-middle-end of their brief lives. Brief, but perfectly lived. There is no room for fiction in the life of the moth; memory is purely genetic, instinctual, factual. A moth never questions the purpose of its life; it lives life as it is meant to, then dies. My husband knows that I like moths; compared to butterflies they seem ancient and wise. I long to feel their wings beat against the palm of my hand, but know how delicate the coloured scales on their wings are, and resist the temptation.

I flick the moth from the paper, into the air outside.

Gloria

Her eyes still closed, she feels for the rounded rim of the bath and holds onto it to steady herself. Eighty-three years ago she was a girl who loved to lie in cooling bath water, prunesoaking, often thinking of her dead mother. She would look down at her chest where young breasts rose like lumps of sourdough – lined up in the cloth-covered pan, they waited in the kitchen for her aunt to put them in the oven.

This is the bath that her granddaughter, Isabel, loved to float in whenever she spent the night, her dark red hair a tangle of seaweed under the water. Its curled feet kept the bath from the floor, providing a good nesting place for snakes. Her aunt had killed a snake in this bathroom when Gloria was eight years old, as she watched, hiding behind her father. He was frozen with fear.

"What a welcome!" Aunt Johanna had said, passing the dead snake to her brother who took it outside with its tail firmly fisted.

It was a baby and they never found the mother.

Lying in the bath, her thoughts became a voiceless language, needing neither tongue, nor words. Steam from the spout of a kettle, obscuring her mother's face. Do I look like her, she wondered. Her aunt's voice intruded: "And who will look after her, now that Elizabeth is gone?"

Gloria tried to speak, but her two tongues twisted like snakes in her throat, choking her. "*Suiplap* father in the kitchen . . . *gemors . . . altyd dors . . .* " she mumbled, rubbing the facecloth over her forehead.

Young Gloria was aware of the spider web in the corner of the bathroom, where no one ever looked and feather dusters couldn't reach. High above her head, where the plaster moulding met the wall, two hunting spiders waited for nightfall, and a meal of moths and gnats.

*

Keeping her eyes closed, Gloria gets up from the toilet and feels her way down the passage to the kitchen. The kettle and a bread bin are standing on a table next to the green velvet chair in which she had breast-fed Ruth seventy-six years before.

She knew she was pregnant when she woke up one morning after a dream that left her feeling seasick. She got up and walked to the kitchen. Poured a small glass of whisky, gulped it down in chinwetting haste. Then made coffee for her husband and carried his cup to the bed, where he hugged secrets of his own as he foetal-curled away from her. She told him, "I must buy a sewing machine . . . that is what mothers do. I will stitch her name in gold and purple on black satin flags."

Frankie took the cup from her just in time, and she ran to the bathroom where she crouched over the porcelain rim of the toilet. Sticky green bile hung from her mouth. She heard her father's voice, "China white mixed with billiard green, neutral in temperature, because of the presence of both warm and cold, binary colour, do you know what I mean by that, child?"

Gloria puts the Bible down next to the kettle, switches it on and feels for a dry crust in the bread bin. Outside the kitchen window she can hear the pigeon she has named Oscar shuffling forward on his red legs. He cocks a red-rimmed eye at her closed lids.

"Here you go," she says, crumbling the crust. "Now shoo, you silly bird!"

A basket of knitting stands next to the chair. She takes a ball of wool and stuffs it into her shirt pocket. A small mirror hangs from a nail just above the kettle. She walks to it and opens her eyes.

"Mirror, mirror on the wall, who is the fairest of them all?" Waits for the answer with her arms crossed.

"Mother," the mirror replies, like it always does.

Steam from the boiling kettle has transformed the mirror into a blank sheet of paper and Gloria takes the corner of a tea towel to clear two spots opposite her eyes. Faceless eyes and no body.

She used to ask the spiders on the ceiling of her childhood bedroom, "What if these are my mother's eyes? Could be, they say I look like her."

Elizabeth's ebony-rimmed mirror still stands facing the bottom of Gloria's bed – when she was young she often stood in front of it, lifting her heavy dark hair from her neck and turning her head from side to side, unburdening her worst fears to the spiders. She stepped close to the mirror, and peered at the large pores of her nose. Her pimpled forehead made her angry. She tried to smooth down her damp hair, always bushing out as it dried, and tossed the haloed frizz over one shoulder. Dark eyebrows lay over lychee pip eyes and she heard her aunt's voice, "You can pluck those when you are older."

She spoke to the eyes in the mirror. "Maybe she is forever trapped in the mirror, where she must have looked at herself in the mornings, in the evenings, and maybe even in between."

Gloria pats her short grey hair and breathes out " . . . hello Mother". The eyes disappear under her hot breath.

Ruth

R uth is thinking of thin slices of Parma ham wrapped around red figs, cinnamon sticks buried in jars of sugar. She is sitting at her kitchen table, staring at her hands. Her laced fingers form a nest. Time seeps through them like a trickle of warm honey, making the table feel sticky.

She can't stop thinking of tonight's farewell; planning it, even though Isabel made it clear from the start that she needed nothing from her.

Fish steaks with macadamias? Potatoes in white wine with anchovies? She gets up to fetch her favourite cookbook, and places it on the table.

Ruth is waiting for time to pass. Waiting for Isabel to arrive to collect a few cases of wine. Waiting for the time to arrive to fetch Gloria and then driving to Morgan's farewell party in McGregor tonight. She is used to waiting. Was always in the kitchen when Isabel returned home from school, dicing, slicing, blanching, cutting, freezing, cooking, boiling, waiting.

She remembers the day Isabel ran into the kitchen, first throwing her school bag down and then her arms around her waist.

"You won't believe what I just saw!" her daughter said, unclasping her hands behind her mother's back, and peering into the mixing bowl on the table.

"There was this accident, I saw it happen. This woman just stopped dead, suddenly, as if seeing a ghost. Her car started spinning, coming straight at me, and I saw her eyes, they were enormous! That's when I noticed the can of tomatoes . . . "

"What can of tomatoes?" Ruth interrupted, thinking that it was really all too much, all those stories and fabrications that crowded in Isabel's head. Cry wolf too often, she thought, and you end up crying over spilt milk.

"Shooting through the air from the back," her daughter continued despite her mother's raised eyebrows, "Hitting her on the back of her head, and her wig flew off – "

"Isabel!"

The low tone of Ruth's voice, dragging the last syllable into a higher register, signalled the familiar warning: Don't go too far, my girl! Don't stretch the truth!

"I saw it happen! I think the wig saved her because the can sliced it from her head, just think how much worse if it hit her head instead!"

Ruth frowned, silenced.

"And then the back door opened, and all her groceries fell out, flour, milk, potatoes, oranges . . . do you think she is dying of cancer and wanted to . . . you know . . . end it all, like Grandma Gloria tries to do all the time?"

Ruth snorted, relieved to find it a pack of lies after all.

"Cancer, my foot. Really, Isabel, where do you get this nonsense from?" Isabel's eyes filled with tears and Ruth handed her a dishcloth.

"Oh, come on, no need to cry," she said, "Did something else happen you're not telling me?" Isabel shook her head, "No, nothing," she said, "But the woman is dead."

"How can you be sure?" Ruth asked, head cocked to one side. Isabel shrugged and walked away.

*

From the top shelf of the broom cupboard Ruth takes a tin of lavender polish and a soft yellow cloth. The lid slips off easily

23

and she lifts a smear onto the cloth. She starts to rub the surface of her kitchen table with small circular movements. Her breasts move under her shirt as she reaches across to the far side of the table; her thighs press against its rounded edge.

The front door bell rings. She leans over the table and looks down the passage. Through the frosted glass panel she sees a dark shape. When she moved from her Muizenberg home she thought she was safe at last from her daily dose of beggars; a steady stream of helpless, hopeless, homeless people in need of money, sugar, bread, coffee.

"No," was her well-practised, standard answer, "I have nothing to give, go to the shelter."

She walks to the front door and opens it without releasing the brass latch-chain.

"Can I help you?" she asks through the slice of open door, barely managing to keep the weary irritation from her voice. The dark-skinned young man smiles. "Ruth?" he asks, "Can I come in?"

Her face colours to a deep shade of red when she realises who he is. Timo, Morgan's young man. Her manner changes from weary suspicion to over-friendly. She slides the chain free and opens the door. "Of course! Come inside, I'll make some tea."

He follows her to the kitchen and picks up the yellow cloth, rubs it hard onto the matt surface of the table. "Ah, this reminds me of when I burnish my pots, I love it. Which is why I will never be a rich man. I get lost in the process and forget about time equals money and all that stuff. I use a small piece of lace agate to burnish; it gives a fantastic, smooth finish."

Ruth has seen some of Timo's coiled pots and doesn't really like them. They look like the bellies of pregnant women, with suggestive mounds indicating buttocks. They make her feel uncomfortable, evoking equal measures of sad longing and distaste.

"But you are making good money with your photography, I hear?" Ruth checks the water level in the kettle, wondering why he has come to see her. A panicked feeling overcomes her and she says, "Is everything okay?" She gives a little laugh, "I mean, it's not as if you pop around every day. Is something wrong with Morgan?"

"Oh no, everything's fine . . . I'm here because Morgan phoned me, or tried to phone me – she kept on breaking up, but I am sure I heard her say that I must come here to fetch something. For tonight's party."

Through the open back door of the kitchen, leading onto a small paved patio, she notices her plants, left where the removal men had placed them three weeks before. Placed randomly, they resemble a huddle of tired, thirsty refugees. On the other side of the rough facebrick wall enclosing her garden a white municipal refuse truck is approaching. They always seem to be in a race against the clock. The driver, barely stopping, teases the workers into a panic that makes them careless. They leave a mess of wet tissues, eggshell and orange rinds behind. Gloria would spit her disgust at their incompetence, lubricating her words with a stream of curses.

"I can't think what it could be she wants. Isabel is coming to fetch some cases of wine from the old cellar in Muizenberg, maybe you misheard?"

He laughs, seemingly unconcerned at the misunderstanding, and the waste of his time. "Well, I'm here now, give me something to do while you make the tea."

"There are the plants," she says, gesturing outside. "They look half dead. I can't remember when I last watered them. Would you mind?"

He walks outside and unrolls the hose from the wall-bracket. Pouring the boiling water onto the swirling tea leaves in the teapot she hears him whistling a jazzy tune, and sees jets of water flit this way and that. Inexplicably, her eyes fill with tears.

"I think they'll survive," he says, coming inside and taking the cup from her.

She picks up the yellow cloth. "Sit down. If you don't mind, I'll carry on with this."

This is also the part she enjoys most, rubbing down hard to bring out the shine. Her wrists hurt but she continues until it is done. She looks up, amazed to find him still there, sitting quietly, holding his cup.

He gets up and takes it to the sink, rinses it and places it on the drying rack. They both turn around to the sound of the ringing telephone. Timo takes his car keys from his pockets and lifts his hand, waves. "Bye," he says, "You get that, I'll let myself out. See you tonight. And thanks for the tea."

*

At least three times a month Frankie would disappear and leave Gloria alone in the house. Urgent telephone calls from an incoherent, or worse, ominously silent Gloria often interrupted Ruth's baking mornings with baby Isabel. She would wave the silent phone in the air towards her baby, supported in her nest of pillows on the table, needing a witness to her suffering.

"Mother . . . is that you?" she always asked, listening to the soft choking sounds coming from Gloria while keeping an eye on Isabel, slowly slipping sideways on the table. Ruth felt a double panic rising: saving mother or saving baby?

"See what I have to put up with," she would tell Isabel, stretching out an arm to steady her as she spoke into the receiver, "God, Mother . . . I don't have time for this!"

She feels that same panic now, listening to the ringing telephone, and hearing the front door slam after Timo's exit.

Ruth wipes at her eyes and picks up the telephone; pulls the yellow cookbook towards her.

"Mom? Where were you? I was worried. I'm going to be a bit late, forgot about Morgan's cat."

"What about Timo? Wasn't he supposed to take it? He just left, maybe Morgan thought the cat was with me."

Ruth opens the cookbook and her eyes stray to a recipe for Gingered Figs. Isabel's voice recedes into the background.

"What? I don't know what you mean. Why would the cat be with you? He's going away for three weeks on a fashion shoot, you know what it's like, last minute decision, and I can't look after Dog for that long. He's leaving tomorrow, after the party. I'm taking it to a cattery this morning on my way to you. But first the roses, I suppose."

Ruth rubs her forehead. Isabel's plans always confuse her, leave her feeling lost. She sighs.

"Do you have any ripe figs?" she asks.

"What? No, it's not fig season, why do you ask?"

"I could bring dessert tonight, at least. Morgan has a sweet tooth, you know."

"I told you I don't need anything, so stop fussing. See you later, okay?"

"I'll see you when I see you, no rush."

Gloria

A tea bag lies at the bottom of the mug. Gloria pours boiling water on top of it, and watches as the water darkens until she cannot see it anymore. She removes the bag with a teaspoon. In the fridge she finds a small carton of milk and adds a drop to her black tea.

A strong smell seeps from a tinfoil-lidded plate, and lifting the foil she reveals two thin slices of cold leftover tongue. It is covered with white mould spots.

"What a treat this was!" She smacks her lips, removing the plate. Pushing it towards the pigeon on the window ledge, she cackles, "Want a bite?"

The pigeon gives her a red-eyed stare, and disappears into a tree. Gloria opens the book-marked Bible and reads out loud, "To keep me from becoming conceited because of these surpassingly great revelations, there was given me a thorn in my flesh, a messenger of Satan to torment me." 2 Corinthians 12:7.

"Do you hear that, Frankie!" she shouts, settling into the chair, spilling hot tea on her arm.

"*Fok!*" she says, the swearword slipping out with a dribble of tea. She always curses in Afrikaans. "*Jirrejesus! Gotinel! Fokinstront!*" God-Jesus, God-in-hell, fuckingshit.

Gloria leans back in the chair and closes her eyes. She sees the young girl sitting up in the bath. The facecloth slips from her breasts and curls back into the water.

She lifts the warm cup of tea to her lips as she remembers the feeling of shrinking, of becoming smaller, that lying in a cold bath created.

She watches the young girl pull a towel from the wooden rail behind the door and slowly wrap it around her disappearing body.

She leans over the bath to pull the plug out.She smoothes the facecloth over the rim of the bath. She turns towards the closed door and opens it.

*

The physical act of knitting now only brings pain. Gloria takes the ball of wool from her pocket and winds it around the needles. With a few stabbing motions she attempts to pull the strand through to create some semblance of cohesion. It resembles Ruth's knitting when she was four years old. The cold steel in her hands, with the wool slipping through her fingers feel familiar, coupled with the taste of tannin on her tongue. Her breasts hang flatly down her chest to just above the small mound of stomach.

Gloria's mind loves playing with numbers and she can make endless sums in her head. They sometimes just go on and on and she doesn't know how to make it all stop. She is a young ninety-six year old, as Dr Roberts puts it.

"Don't get fresh with me, young man," she told him then, "You are young enough to be my son." At seventy, he certainly is. He is long retired and Gloria is his only patient.

More numbers and dates tumble into her head, unbidden. 1949. 1919. 1975. 1903. 1924. 1944. A small 8 creeps in. It has a dark fringe and dark eyes. She hears the shutter-click of a camera, hears the hissing of the flash bulb, as it illuminates the face of her granddaughter.

Her hand tightens its grip on the needles, and she feels for her cup of tea.

Birthdates, death dates. It doesn't matter which is which – in a way they are interchangeable.

3, 16, 5, 20, 5, 10, 16, 7. The years between births and deaths. She can't have her own death, but no one can stop her from thinking about those of others.

There are three years between Gloria's birth and that of Frankie, who was born first.

Five years separate her son-in-law David from Ruth.

Gloria was only sixteen years old when the husband of her yet unconceived daughter was born.

She takes a sip of cold tea, her head spinning. Past meeting present, blurring into the future.

Half the gene pool that would one day form her granddaughter was already suckling at his mother's breast, far away in Scotland, when Gloria was still a young girl with newly functioning ovaries and an irregular menstrual rhythm.

Over the past ten years Gloria has become selective in her hearing – choosing when to play deaf, and when to hear. She turns her hearing aid right down in certain company, and full volume in others. This keeps everyone on their toes.

Some days she hears nothing at all.

Isabel was ten years old when Frankie died, Gloria suddenly remembers. But hadn't she heard Frankie snoring an hour ago, next to her in bed? She looks down the dark passage towards her bedroom door, panic drying her mouth.

Morgan

I cross the dark brown water of the Breede River on the way to my mother's farm just outside the town of McGregor, which lies 230km east of Cape Town. The car is fully laden with crates of books and rock samples, its chassis sunk low. The riverbank is the setting for enthusiastic baptisms, and driving home on Sunday the screams of young women, emerging from the brown water, will spill into my car. My empty car, with tonight's farewell party a memory to keep me company.

Today the flanks of the mountain on my left are barren and rocky, but every winter hundreds of aloe plants erupt in a glory of red flames, as Grandpa David put it, turning the mountain red.

"It reminds me of a skinned and bleeding beast," Isabel said when I told her about David's comment.

"Why do you always have to be so melodramatic?" I asked, knowing she had no way of answering. My mother was busy pulling clumps of knotted hair from her brush, throwing them into the wastebasket in her bathroom.

"I see what I see. I can't help it," she replied, washing her hands.

I imagine the red strokes of colour waiting to emerge after the first winter rain as I pass the row of sawn-off Bluegum stumps. Slender new trees are growing from each of them.

The house appears as if by magic, as it always does when my car rounds the last corner of the road. It nestles low into the mountain, sunk into the landscape. The lavender bushes on

31

either side of the road seem to wait, their fragrant purple laps falling open.

The tracks on the steep slope of the hill, leading to the house, are overgrown with weeds. I crawl up slowly in first gear, then stop in the shade of the Karoo willow I planted with my father twenty years ago. I get out and inhale the peppery smell of Karoo vegetation.

A wild fennel patch, planted by my mother to chase away kitchen flies, obscures a large *Aloe ferox* at the start of the stone labyrinth.

"Aloes are God's spirit soldiers," my grandfather once said as he carried one, bought at the nursery in Robertson, from his car, "I think it will be a fitting marker for the start of our labyrinth."

Aloes bring back memories of standard eight biology, and early morning car trips to school with my mother.

In an unspoken agreement we honoured a truce in the mornings on the way to school. Sitting next to her in the car I revised my biology lessons by reading sections out loud. My mother was my captive audience.

"A plant's stem supports its buds, leaves and flowers. Inside the stem cells . . . inside the stem *are* cells that carry water, minerals, and food to different parts of the plant. Roots anchor the plant and absorb water and minerals . . . "

Sometimes I continued silently in my head, but my mother would nudge me with her elbow, saying, "Come on, tell me more, it's very interesting."

"Chloroplasts . . . where the food is made . . . mesophyll palisade . . . tightly packed . . . stomata . . . "

She often interrupted, mid-stream.

"What are stigmata in plants? Are they wounds?"

"Not stigmata Mom, sto-mata. They're very small pores . . . microscopically small . . . on the underside of leaves, that allow carbon dioxide and oxygen to pass in and out the leaf. Don't you know about photosynthesis and all that stuff?"

"I forgot it all, except for unconnected bits. I know that plants absorb red and blue light, and reflect green. That's why they appear green, but it's an illusion."

My mother loved to talk about what was real and what was not, of what appeared real and what was merely an illusion. Unfortunately, the school system demanded a firm grasp of facts, and I told her so.

"Don't confuse me! My teacher isn't interested in illusions, she wants facts."

She just nodded her head, waving me on, "Go on, I won't interrupt again."

"Wood consists of layers of xylem cells toughened with a substance called lignin. Each growing season a new ring of xylem is added, forming tree rings."

"Middle-age spread," my mother interrupted.

"What?"

I wanted to scream at her. "*Please* just let me finish this section, we're almost there."

I close my eyes and conjure up a section from my school textbook.

"The Aloe can exist under extremely dry conditions. It is a xerophytic plant . . . adventitious roots rise from its base . . . the leaves are spirally arranged on the stem . . . the leaf bases form a sheath around the stem . . . "

Isabel isn't here now, ready to interrupt, to ask questions.

"What's that? Adventitious? Xerophytic? How do you manage to remember all these strange names?"

Isabel

I follow the cat's meowing to my daughter's old bedroom. "Kitty-kitty-kitty! Dog, where are you? Come on out cat, I don't have all day."

Dog moves from under the bed towards the bowls of water and food I put down on the carpet.

Herinnering aan jou is opgekerf. I sit down on my daughter's bed and look around at the few bits and pieces still waiting to be collected. Cut-up memories of my daughter are distributed throughout the house. A guitar, a basket filled with rolled-up posters of horses and handsome cricketers, a row of blue and green bottles standing on her desk. Next to them stands a jam jar filled with the beads she slid from the cut strings of all the necklaces she loved to wear as a teenager.

"You could restring them," I said, "Make something new."

"No," she answered, "You can have them."

A week before she moved out of this house and into the one she built with Timo, I entered her room, looking for a book of mine she'd never returned. A fashion magazine lay on her bed, and I picked it up wondering if Timo's work was featured inside. Four photographs tumbled out and fell to the floor. As I picked them up, Morgan came in and grabbed them from me.

"Were you snooping in my bedroom? Why are you in here?"

"Looking for my *Poisonwood Bible*," I said.

"You could've just asked," she looked down at the photographs, blushing, "Did you look at these?"

"I saw them as they fell out. Did Timo take them?"

"Of course!"

"I didn't mean to snoop . . . bad hiding place, if you ask me – "

She threw the photographs onto the bed, "I wasn't hiding them, I'm not ashamed! Look all you want!" The door slammed behind her as she left the room.

I shuffled the photographs back into a pile. The top one showed Morgan naked, leaning back against a rock. Her eyes met the gaze of the camera; her mouth was curved into a seductive smile. One hand fanned open fingers over the dark triangle between her legs; the other gently cupped a breast. I pushed them back between the pages of the magazine, erasing the memory of that other set of photographs where my own eyes stared back at me.

*

I get up from her bed and close the door behind me to prevent the cat's escape.

The door to Jonathan's study is open and I walk to the bookshelf to take out the copy of a beautifully illustrated nineteenth-century botanical atlas. The relief I had first felt at giving birth to a healthy baby soon wore off, and was replaced by endless sunspeckled dustmote time spent looking after Morgan. No one bothered to tell me that babysouls were vampires that devoured those of their mothers. Like my daughter's thick cotton diapers, time became soaked through with her needs.

"Why don't you leave her with David and Ruth sometimes, or get a babysitter – get back to work," Jonathan suggested, often. Back then, not even I understood my refusal to do so.

A beam of illuminated dust entered our living room window at nine o'clock in mid-summer, much later in winter, and became the compass of my day. I watched as Morgan tried to catch the golden dust with her small jam tart hands, aware of a steady trickle of brain cells oozing out of my head. I realised then that there are those who find themselves when they have children, and those who lose themselves.

With Morgan hip-grafted, I walked into Jonathan's study and paged through the botanical books on the shelves. I started playing games with words I found in these books, while Morgan played with ribbons of dust and bright wooden blocks and paint and mud. Drawn to their sturdy spines, to the facts contained between the serious covers. As if it was possible, through osmosis, to find myself another life. Opening them at random to read the strangely moving sentences out loud into the baby-sleep air, I transformed random passages into poetry.

Between the pages of the atlas I find a long-forgotten poem.

Two diatom beside each other
surrounded themselves
with glutinous mass.
The valves then fell apart
like an opened book.
The contents of each other
come together, but do not mix.

Next, the two contents
clothe themselves
with a delicate membrane.

Words like *zygospore, frustulia, myxomycetes* and *euglena* rolled around in my head like shiny satin balls. Random pages and random passages became random destiny: the words my finger chose were the blessing for the day. Closing my eyes, I place my finger on the page. Under a section on the male shield fern I finger my destiny.

The young fronds are rolled up like a shepherd's crook, and gradually unfold themselves.

Morgan

The fennel plants have grown into two-metre high monsters, obscuring the start of the labyrinth. I bend down and pull the roots of the smallest one free. Shaking the loose soil from the roots I remember that the ovary of an aloe is trilocular, a. three-chambered heart.

My best friend, Ana, whose father was a gynaecologist, informed me of the existence of my own ovaries. We shared reproductive information long before my mother had her little talk with me, and gave me a book that I never bothered to read.

Ana and I looked at diagrams of sexual intercourse, crudely copied from her father's textbooks. Also at drawings of the male and female reproductive systems. The word *penetration* was inexplicably exciting. Even the instruction leaflet tucked inside a box of tampons caused fits of embarrassed giggles. Huddling together in a corner of the athletics field under the deep purple shadows of a Jacaranda tree, Ana and I recoiled from the brutal appearance of the reptile that was called *erect penis*. We decided never to have sex, or intercourse, still believing it to be two different actions. The one for fun, which only movie-stars enjoyed, the other to make babies, which is what our parents did, once, before we were born.

*

I designed the labyrinth to start level with the ground, slowly increasing in height through its scrolling path. Walking through it gives the sensation of sinking into soft sand, as the ever-higher wall blocks out more and more of the landscape until only sky remains.

"Redemption, salvation, freedom," Grandpa David had said as he watched me place stone after stone onto the hard McGregor soil. "The journey to God leads one not to God, but to a place free from wanting God, or needing God. Is that what you are trying to tell me?"

"No-o, I don't think so . . . but it seems to be what you need to hear."

I stood back and admired my handiwork. My grandfather stood next to me and said, "The mazes on the floors of medieval churches were supposed to remind the faithful of the convoluted journey of the Christian soul to salvation. A wrong turn could result in being lost forever. I think that's why it was the right decision to build a labyrinth, not a maze. There is only one entry and one exit. All you need to do is follow the path."

"Why did you leave Grandma?" I asked, wanting to catch him unprepared. He bent down and shifted the last stone I had placed a little to the left.

"I will tell you when I find out. All I know is that God hides from me when I am with Ruth."

"Or maybe you are the one hiding," I answered, which made him smile.

"I did have a dream last night," he said, "Which has made me think. It had something to do with a celibate priest, rubbing make-up – you know, that beige stuff you women use – over his stubble, but roughly, and unevenly, as if he wanted me to notice what he was hiding, or denying."

"Did he say anything to you?"

"No. I was aware, while dreaming, of being in a soundless space. The priest and I never spoke, but I felt disturbed by him, by his melancholy sadness, I suppose. Anyway, it's still with me. Strange how some dreams are like that."

"Are *you* celibate?" I wanted to ask, but didn't. I wasn't prepared to start a conversation about my grandfather's sex life.

For two weeks, before settling on the final design, he traced a new labyrinth every day against the mountain slope outside the house, using, round white river stones.

"Labyrinth walking is about letting go," I instructed him, "Allowing the path to find you, not the other way around."

In the evenings I made the cooking fire while he walked through his latest labyrinth tracing. He carried a notebook and pen with him, and a measuring tape in his pocket.

"You cannot understand this mathematically," I told him, but he continued to take down measurements, and making small adjustments to the curving paths.

After supper we sat in silence and watched the moon as it rose over the mountain, illuminating the white stones.

I put a stalk of fennel in my mouth and it fills with the familiar liquorice taste of childhood holidays.

In the field to my left a cow stands, left there for the night to graze. She has managed to wrap the piece of sisal rope hanging from her neck around the trunk of an olive tree, and is kneeling in awkward prayer. I bend down and release her before unlocking the back door.

Isabel

B ack in my bedroom I take a book from the top of the pile and open it. My eyes catch one sentence: "Inverness, a small town containing trout and Highlanders, is built entirely of pink granite."

Die dorpie Inverness is vol Highlanders en forelle. Die hele dorp is gebou met pienk graniet.

In my mother tongue it sounds like pure fantasy, a small sugar-town that belongs in the tale of Hansel and Gretel.

"Liar, liar, pants on fire, your nose is as long as a telephone wire!" The taunting rhyme from my childhood haunts me, for, as I have always known, a thin line separates fact from fiction.

I pick up the Gaelic-English dictionary I found at a second-hand bookstore recently: *Faclair Gàidhlig – Beurla*. Opening it, I read a list of words out loud – "*Bas, bàs, bàsaich, bas-bhualadh, beannachd –* " – feeling like a two-year-old trying to read Ruth's cookbooks while watching her stir, pour, knead, cut.

"You always sniffed and licked my recipes," Ruth told me later, "As if you thought the words were part of the ingredients."

Thoughts of my mother remind me to phone her and I lift the receiver to dial her new telephone number. Her phone rings, and when she eventually answers she sounds upset.

"Mom? Where were you? I was worried. I'm going to be a bit late, forgot about Morgan's cat." It doesn't take long before she starts to talk about food, insisting on baking something for tonight's party. I feel her slip away, not hearing a word I say.

My love affair with words began in my mother's kitchen. Words became creatures, like the one-eyed monster of *rib-eye steak.*

41

"My mother knows a tribe of people who removed one eye from their enemies, and then cooked these eyes on an open fire," I told Sarie, entering the kitchen one morning after she had slept over at my house. I took out a bowl of lychees from the fridge and passed it to her, "This vicious tribe left one eye in the heads of their victims, so that they were forced to watch their captors eat the meal of steamed eyes."

Sarie's hands were clasped over her mouth; holding her breath and shaking her head from side to side. She declined my offer of lychees and yoghurt for breakfast.

"That's where the saying *an eye for an eye* comes from," I continued, "This is the same tribe of people who peel and cook the tongues of calves."

Sarie screamed as I popped a lychee in my mouth.

"Would you like blueberry pancakes for breakfast?" my mother asked as she entered the kitchen, walking to the sink. She bent down to fetch a pan in the cupboard underneath.

The word *blueberry* was a flat sweet cloud floating the evil tribe away.

*

As I walk from my bedroom, my head fills with an image of a rose-tinted city. Its inhabitants are plotting and scheming in an incomprehensible tongue to steal my daughter's heart.

Locking the front door and placing the keys in my pocket, I walk down the seven stone steps onto the tar pavement.

A gust of wind closes the green garden door behind me.

Ruth

Drops of sun drip from the tap with the worn washer, splashing sparkles of light into the kitchen sink. A collection of knives rests blade-down inside a tall ceramic holder standing on the counter next to the sink.

She turns from the phone and puts the yellow cloth and the purple tin into the broom cupboard. With Timo gone the room feels too empty, too silent. She tries to whistle, like he did, but even though no one is there to hear, she blushes at the sounds that flute from her puckered lips. Silence is preferable, she thinks, and spreads an old sheet, folded double, over the table. She tips the contents of her cutlery drawers onto the white surface, and, walking around the table, starts sorting it into different piles. Much like an archaeologist would do after a successful day's digging.

Knives, spoons, forks. Then classifies even further: the knives into small piles of steak, fish, butter, chopping, carving, slicing, paring. The forks into cake, fish, meat. Spoons into piles of soup, dessert and tea. She finds a single serrated grapefruit spoon and places it next to a small silver mustard spoon.

Looking at the arsenal of knives spread out on her table, she thinks of the thin tracks of blood that she found on Gloria's wrists once, made with the tip of a boning knife over her purple veins. Ruth wrapped them with bandages, asking, "For God's sake, Mother, get a grip. Did you really think this feeble effort could kill you?"

"Of course not," Gloria's answered, "Once I thought of the mess, I couldn't go through with it. Couldn't do that to you . . . you should thank me for it."

Ruth's hands gripped the handle of Isabel's pushchair when they walked home. She told her sleeping daughter about barbiturates and gin, and her grandmother's head stuck in a gas oven, passed out and peaceful.

*

Three weeks ago Ruth had everybody over for a last meal at the large house in Muizenberg before moving to this flat in Kenilworth.

Gloria was asleep in a chair, clutching her red notebook filled with the names of colours. Ruth watched as Isabel slid it from her fingers and sat down next to her grandmother. She paged through the notebook and attempted to count the colours named. The words were crammed together in a spiderscript.

"Just listen to some of these," her daughter called out., "Oatcake, Wheat Germ, Fresh Drop, Apple Sauce, Pleasant and Wax Bean. Who gets paid to think up all of this?"

"Well, she gets them from hardware stores, from those little cardboard strips. There are thousands of names for all the different shades of paint," Ruth said, walking over to Isabel, who placed the notebook next to the plastic beaker Gloria used for her weak solution of tea and whisky.

Jonathan was looking through a box filled with books. He glanced at his watch and Ruth saw that he was impatient to get home. She handed him Gloria's plate with a few slices of braised tongue under dollops of mustard and cream sauce. Her mother's favourite. "Take this to her, would you?" she asked, and then carried one dish after the other between kitchen and dining room.

"I can't believe how well the farm stall down the road is doing, all those women buying pre-cooked meals . . . but it's just not the same, even though it says 'home-cooked' on the box. How can it be? Anonymous cooks cooking for people they'll never meet. Mass produced."

Morgan and Timo walked in from outside and joined Jonathan at the table. Ruth put down a dish of glazed sweet potato, next to a platter holding a herbed loin of lamb. Isabel sat down next to Timo and asked, "How would you translate the Afrikaans word *bredie?*"

"Stew," he said, taking the platter of sweet potatoes from Ruth.

"I didn't make a *bredie* today, if that's what you are asking," Ruth interrupted, "Only what you see on the table. And it didn't turn out so well."

She turned to Timo. "I can't seem to get it right anymore. Not like when my husband was alive, he really enjoyed a dish of sweet potatoes. Had the leftovers with cinnamon sugar, after."

"It looks the same to me," Isabel said, lifting a portion into her plate. "It smells the same . . . and probably tastes the same."

"Well, you've always been easy to please." Ruth wiped at the wetness on her cheeks with her oven gloves.

"I never got over your father leaving me like that," she said, "And I never will. And now Morgan is leaving as well."

"Oh Gran, not you as well, it's hard enough as it is!"

Morgan stood up and hugged Ruth, taking the dish from her. "Sit down and enjoy yourself."

She passed the sweet potatoes to Jonathan, and pushed the lamb on its large white platter towards Ruth. It was deboned, rolled around a rosemary, garlic and thyme stuffing.

Gloria watched from the chair, licking her lips. Her hands rested next to her plate, on top of the metal TV tray Jonathan had placed in front of her. She closed her eyes and drifted off.

"You carve, Gran, we can't mess with tradition now." Ruth stood up and took the knife from Morgan.

"Out of the blue, a man his age, did he think he could find happiness out there when, after fifty-five years of marriage, he hasn't managed to find it *in here?*" she said, tapping her breastbone with the handle of the carving knife.

Isabel

L ately every day has begun with a promise of rain, carried on the fierce breath of bergwinds. Several birds are hovering over the workmen, curious to see how their landscape is being changed. A clump of greyheaded gulls land and stare with heads tilted, strangely cat-like.

A human chain of hands throws stones into waiting wire baskets, forming retaining walls; bales of hay are opened and spread out in a bleak yellow band on the opposite bank of this new river to weigh down the sand particles. The sound of the large front-loaders and scrapers temporarily blocks out the shush of the sea.

I cross the railway line and step onto the beach. The sea lies to my left and the railway line to my right. At the start of my walk I have the sun at my back, and on the return journey I squint at its brightness. My beach walk is a ritual passage on familiar ground and I hardly notice sea or sky or sand anymore. Lately, I feel the stubs of unborn wings nestling under my shoulder blades. They enfold and hold the moment of death for a moth, a moment that has stayed with me since Jonathan's moth-telling.

"The Silver Spotted Ghost moth scatters its seeds in flight," Jonathan told me last night to cheer me up. "Not a moment's maternal care."

As a child I believed that moth-souls resembled an endless stream of small Brazilian pepper tree flowers, light green and waxy, like the ones that sifted down to the ground in the back garden of my grandfather's house. I wondered if a dying moth merely becomes still, or spread its wings, if it had them, one last time before falling off the branch as dust.

That tree was capable of telling the time, and my clock was tuned to its inner rhythms while the grown-ups argued under its shade. Bees arrived early in the morning to drink their fill, and to pollinate. The tree hummed and shimmered all through the morning. It became quiet when the sun was directly overhead, and the sudden silence was my reminder to run inside for lunch.

The lunch my grandfather prepared tasted different to my mother's adventurous cooking; her expert blending of spices and herbs replaced by his careless sprinkling of salt and pepper. His food made my eyes water, and the taste lingered on my tongue long after Ruth fetched me from my grandparent's house, and took me home.

My grandfather, Frankie, died a month after I witnessed the death of a bald woman in a car accident. As I stopped to stare, the hubcap fell from the front wheel of her car and spun drunkenly past me, collapsing against the curb. A man came running from a nearby house. All the buttons were missing from his cardigan, which threatened to slip from his shoulders as he ran back into his house to call the ambulance. His long legs reminded me of my grandfather, who was lying in a hospital bed, still alive but waiting to die. He also liked to wear open cardigans, with buttons hanging loose-necked from their threads.

The driver's door swung open, and I saw blood on the inside, splattered against the pale blue vinyl. A blonde wig was hooked over the chrome window handle; I almost mistook it for a scalped head. Groceries tumbled out the open back door – a split pack of flour, a different brand to the one my mother used, a bag of oranges, intact. Potatoes lay like lumpy stones across the road. Five tins of tomatoes followed in the path of the hubcap.

I didn't want to look at the woman trapped behind the steering wheel. Her hand reached for the wig, trying to pull it from the handle. I heard her voice, calling out, and turned around to run home as fast as I could. The tall man came rushing from his house, with a blanket in his hand. As I passed him I saw that he had taken his cardigan off, and rolled up the sleeves of his shirt.

If I'd thought that the woman had seen me standing and staring, I would have had no choice but to go to her, and help her put her wig back on her head.

Instead I ran as fast as I could, with the refrain of a familiar fantasy beating through the fear and shame I felt at abandoning the bald woman. All I wanted was to run home to the safety of my mother's kitchen.

Tell-her-tell-her-tell-her, I thought as I ran, but after a while, with pounding heart and pounding feet, it sounded just like *liar, liar, liar, liar.*

I wanted to tell my mother everything. About my grandmother's eyes, looking at me from behind a lace curtain, and of the pointy ivy leaves pressing into my back, pushed against the hedge at the bottom of their garden, and my grandfather's hot breath in my ear, but she was busy cooking when I arrived. Her hands were hidden in the cream-coloured mixing bowl and she lifted the sticky mess for me to see, raising her shoulders. I walked to her and hugged her around her waist. Bits of dough fell on my hair.

Tell-her-liar-tell-her, I thought, but she started speaking first, measuring out more flour to add to the sticky mixture inside the bowl.

"Always measure dry first, then wet," she reminded me, as if we had spent the morning in a cooking class, as if I hadn't just seen a woman die. Surely no one can survive the loss of so much blood.

"You look funny," she said, and peered at me with her eyebrows raised, "Did something happen at school?"

"You won't believe it," I said, and told my mother every thing I had seen.

Gloria

Gloria's father, Patrick, was away when she was born, selling art materials to artists living in remote villages along the southern Cape coastline. He was receiving secret painting lessons from an old woman living in a stone cottage in the village of Waenhuiskrans. Once a year he spent a week with her, painting a self-portrait, and then taking home the portrait he had painted the previous year. In 1902 he painted the face of his wife, and took it home after the following year's trip. He arrived home to news of his daughter's birth, and the death of his wife.

Gloria's birth pangs interrupted Elizabeth, holding a brush loaded with the blue she desired so desperately. She lapped it up with her eyes as she squeezed it from the tube and into the tin of house paint. She stepped down from the ladder, her skirt tucked into her underpants, and twisted her ankle.

He wasn't there when the brush slipped from her hand, splashing blue drops onto her legs. The last stroke on the cupboard dried, unfinished, with ridged bristle marks.

She emptied her bladder in the chamber pot under her bed and lay down. Then turned her face towards the sea, and watched the full moon detach from the dark horizon, like a single cell escaping a larger organism. As Patrick's sister, Johanna, entered with the midwife, Elizabeth noticed the moon float away into the waiting space of sky with an urgency and speed that seemed to match that of her unborn daughter's arrival. She kept her eyes on the moon, lying back on wet pillows, exhausted.

A delicate web of organic matter, like the patterning of decalcified bone, danced in front of her eyes, blue-speckled. The smell of linseed oil was in the air. Hands tugged at her limbs, a wet towel was placed on her brow. She heard women's voices, saw their words dropping into a pond, like stones, *pushnow! pushnow!* rippling out a meaning, amplifying until she almost understood, but always retreating a moment too soon.

The silent moonpath across the water illuminated a woman in a white veil walking towards the edge of the sea. Her feet were encrusted with small snail-shells, and as she sank beneath the waves her veil floated up to the surface of the foamy sea.

Lace on lace.

*

The hot sun on her cheek wakes Gloria. The tea has gone cold on the low table next to her, and the nest of knitting has slipped from her lap and is lying on the floor. Through the kitchen window she sees the sea's tidal markings, crested wave turned into foamy scum on the sand.

Uitgespoel en verby, she thinks, as she struggles out of the green chair, stiff-limbed after the long sit, and shuffles to the bedroom. Over and done with.

The dream she had walks with her down the passage.

There was a beach. A house. Water. She was inside the house, sleeping. Frankie was next to her, snoring and maybe also dreaming. Where is Frankie now, she wonders. Now that she is finally ready to talk to him, now that knowledge has become a lump, a growth in her throat.

"Where are you now, Frankie?" she shouts, her voice old, scared.

"Is this why I can't die? God, please just let me die!"

Her shout turns into a coughing fit and she holds onto the door-frame to catch her breath.

The quilt is lying on the floor where she kicked it. She steps over it and gets into bed, under the cool cotton sheet; stretches her arm over to Frankie's side. Even after death, after almost forty years, still Frankie's side. She opens her fingers like a fan on his smooth pillow, breathing in and breathing out; finally sleeps.

Next to her lies a woman in a white veil. She is also sleeping. She is holding Gloria's right hand with her left hand.

They share the same dream. In this dream a woman is sitting next to the lifeless body of her mother. Her mother has been dead for some time, and her corpse is beginning to blacken. Her daughter knows that she must wash her, and prepare her for her grave, but she feels repulsed and scared. She has left it too late and now the task seems unbearable.

In the dream Gloria sighs, and thinks, I can't do this. My only way out of this is if I die too.

She lies down next to the rotten corpse of her mother and waits to die.

The ceiling fan that David installed for her squeaks through its slow circular path.

Isabel

Shoreline predators share my morning walk and they all approach their prey in different ways. Some sit and wait, some are active hunters, and some scavenge on weak or dead animals.

A foamy splash of wave forces me onto a heap of kelp, whose roots are home to clusters of mussels and concertina-shaped clams. I bend down and tug tentatively, testing their tenacity. They are clinging on for dear life. These roots are a fitting home for my grandmother. A teeming, throbbing place where a heart can barely survive.

I grew from that coil of umbilical matter, a tall stalk swaying perilously in the cold water of memory.

Narrow kelp leaves, transformed into dark punctuation marks by their air-filled bladders, are tossed out on the beach. They shout urgent messages that dissolve into sea mist before I can hear them. I often misread signs, like the one at a parking garage in Muizenberg warning against illegal parking: "No barking, hermits only."

"Scene of the grime," I told my mother whenever we visited Gloria, and cleaned her kitchen.

My mother passed me a handful of wet knives to dry. "Never point a knife at someone, always pass it holding the blade with the handle pointing towards them." She seemed unconcerned that the blade would then be pointing at her heart. "And don't ever receive a knife as a gift, if you do, always give a coin in return."

"Why?" I asked.

"A knife given as a gift will lead to a quarrel. You have to turn it into a purchase. Your Scottish granny believed it and so should you."

The warm wind coming from the mountain spices the early autumn chill. My fellow walkers move past me with hands thrust into pockets, bracing for the rain that threatens from the south.

When I was nine years old I overheard my mother use the phrase "molecular weight". We were visiting one of her friends and I slipped away to find the kitchen, as was my habit when visiting other homes. I sat down in front of the stove and repeated it over and over as if it was the key to an important riddle. I wondered if one could measure the molecular weight of blood, and noticing a kitchen scale, I imagined it filled with red foamy bubbles; membrane-sealed puffs of air. The needle of the scale rested on 0. The molecular weight of blood, I decided, was zero.

During my many mornings alone in kitchens while my mother drank tea under trees, talking to friends, I glimpsed past kitchen-happenings. Frozen slices of other lives. Saw other mothers seated at tables, cooking-baking-waiting. Kitchen knives spread out on kitchen tables – small sharp ones with stout black handles, and large ones that reminded me of ragged-tooth sharks.

I liked to lie under tables, staring up at the unvarnished, unpolished and unpainted surfaces that no one ever thought about. When I closed my eyes I could see my mother holding a blue and silver tin, tilting a creamy liquid from it onto an orange cloth.

"Please-please let me!" I whined as she rubbed the liquid onto the waiting knives, spread out on the white sheet on the table. I can see her now, frozen in that moment of waiting with her arms outstretched, holding cloth and tin, until the shiny surfaces were powdery and dulled. The tips of her fingers held the knives down as she smeared the grey powder onto the sheet below. It formed dark shadows that surrounded an army of silver knives when she lifted the sheet to the light.

When I finally moved out of my parents' house, I wanted to take my mother's kitchen with me. Especially the smells. What I really wanted was a scratch-and-smell motherkitchen with the aromas of cinnamon and lemon and danhia and butternut.

My grandmother's kitchen was different. On the mornings my parents left me with her I spent most of my time hiding.

"She has been good for a while now," I heard my mother say to my father, "She is trying hard to behave . . . we have to show Gloria that we trust her."

I crouched in the shadows, watching my grandmother. She sat behind an old-fashioned and clumsy pair of scales, weighing out ingredients to bake a cake. A lilac shawl was draped over a purple blouse. The fringe was wet and sticky with clumps of beaten egg-white. She reached for a pack of flour, but her hand slipped and she spilled it in a creamy cloud. A strand of hair from her face kept bothering her, and just as I was about to emerge from the shadow behind the door to help, she wiped it away, leaving a dusting of flour on her long lashes. They looked like cow's eyelashes, sticking out from her eyelids in a stiff, straight fringe. When she took the cake from the oven it sloped sideways, like the foot of a mountain meeting the sea.

*

It is shark egg season on the beach. Every step I take reveals a cluster of stripy black and ivory mermaid's purses. Some shark species, like cat- and nursehound sharks, deposit their eggs in crevices when the cases are still soft – this way, there's a chance of their remaining stuck and safe from predators until they hatch.

"Doesn't the mother look after her babies?" Morgan once asked, busy researching her standard one shark project.

"No, they don't need to."

"Oh look," she said, showing me a photograph, "The baby sharks use special skin teeth to tear the capsule open, and can look after themselves."

Empty whelk and cone shells line the windowsill of my kitchen, hunters turned into trophies. Looking at them when I do the day's dishes, I think of the arsenal of weaponry those shells conceal.

Sulphuric acid pours from the proboscis of many whelk species, as the creature dissolves its meal before ingesting it. Starfish use their tube feet to tear the valves of mussels apart. If that fails, it turns its stomach inside out and pours a muscle-relaxant fluid over the mussel, causing it to open up.

A few shark egg purses on the beach this morning have tiny holes through which a predator sucked the baby before it could be born. Others show signs of a successful escape. I hold one up to the light and see that it is a beautiful resinous sea-amber.

A dead ladybird is caught in the strong pale tendrils, a passenger hitching a ride.

Gloria

Morgan's voice wakes her. "You can't mess with tradition now," she says, and the dream image of Frankie, standing on the balcony attached to the bedroom of their Worcester home, fades away. His mouth was sewn closed with thick black thread.

Gloria turns slowly onto her back. Sweat slides from her hairline into her left ear. Her cheek is embossed with the pattern of a leaf embroidered on the pillowcase under her head.

Seventy-six years ago she had lain on this bed, fear beating out a rhythm over her stretched belly, thinking of her aunt's words, "Your mother died giving birth to you. Your head got stuck. We told her to push, not to give up, but she did. There was blood everywhere, we had to drag you out, limb by limb."

Gloria's baby pushed against the wall of her womb, and the knitting needles slipped from her hands. The embroidered cushion on the chair was soaked through. She shouted into the empty house, even though she knew that Frankie was not home yet. She imagined his long legs straddling his office chair, saw him straightening piles of paper on his pale wooden desk. Anger at Frankie's absence increased the intensity of the contractions, and she knelt down with her ripe belly touching the floor.

"I don't want to die, I don't want to die," she whispered, her breath stirring the dust on the floor.

Firesparkles formed in front of her eyes. Her mother's chair, along with her bed, moved with Gloria to her new house in Worcester, a silent observer in the corner. Its back was covered with Frankie's cardigan, limp arms sweeping the floor.

Outside the window she could hear birds fighting over a meal.

She lifted her head and looked up at the ceiling; hissed hot breath at the spiders, wondering what she looked like, to them. Wondering if her mother had also seen spiders on a ceiling, just before she died.

A key turned in the door and Gloria screamed louder. Frankie's footsteps fell faster along the passage. She heard the jingle of keys as he threw them down. The sound echoed from far away. His legs appeared, the fabric stretched across his thighs; his braces were hooked over his shoulders, two thin red snakes disappearing into the overgrowth of his cotton shirt. Large, to hide the shortness of his upper body.

His nails scratched the skin of her upper arms as he pulled her up and onto the bed. The midwife arrived just in time to hand over the slippery bundle, flesh from Gloria's flesh, still attached to the purple cord. Frankie cowered in the corner of the room peeping from behind splayed fingers.

The midwife took the baby away, and Frankie sat down on the chair. He stroked the nails of his right hand with the tip of his left index finger, then curled his fingers into the palm of his hand until his knuckles turned yellow. When he opened his hand, small purple slashes lay across the lines of heart, life, and fate.

He didn't look at his daughter. She was lying in the arms of the midwife, who exclaimed how beautiful she was. Gloria held out her arms.

"I must go now," Frankie said, white and damp-faced, "I left the office early, there is unfinished business."

"Let me look at her," Gloria reached out, and took her baby from the woman. She rested her fingers lightly on the softly pulsing spot at the top of her daughter's head.

"Your name is Ruth," she said, and Frankie looked up.

"That's a bit Biblical don't you think?"

"Well . . . you never know. He may exist, after all, how can I be sure?"

His office was waiting, the glass paperweights waiting to reflect small round distortions of him into the room. Waiting for him to move the one on his left a fraction to the right, and to sit back with a sigh.

"The office needs me," he said again, fingering the pen in his breast pocket, his jacket already hanging from his narrow shoulders. He imagined the meticulous entries he would make in his red notebook.

Birth of my daughter, Ruth. 2 September, 1924. Eye-colour not yet determined, most likely brown. Dark hair. Small mouth. GOBB.

"Go," Gloria told him, stroking the top of Ruth's head, "Just go."

*

Gloria turns on her side and hugs Frankie's pillow to her stomach.

"Just go," she breathes into the soft body of the pillow, "Go."

Morgan

The taste of fennel still on my tongue, I open the back door and walk into the kitchen, where the cool darkness is a relief after the hot two-hour drive. This house will serve as a memory chest to keep the things I cannot take with me to Scotland.

I put my bag down on the table that spans the length of the room, and open the tap of the basin under the window. The water from the tap is pale amber; I drink a bitter mouthful and splash my face. Through the window I can see the cow, grazing contentedly.

My bedroom is at the end of the passage. Both walls are covered with paintings, a row of ten on one wall, eleven on the opposite one. They are small, about thirty-by-thirty centimetres. There are twenty portraits of Gloria's father, Patrick, and one of his wife, Elizabeth. They seem to be painted by the same artist. My mother thinks that they were in lieu of payment for Patrick's art materials. When Ruth moved into her small flat Isabel brought the portraits here.

Viewed from the kitchen it seems as if Patrick is looking at the faded blue cupboard where we keep the crockery. My grandmother Ruth told me that her grandmother, Elizabeth, had been busy painting this cupboard just before she gave birth to Gloria, Ruth's own mother.

The portraits are not signed, only dated. Elizabeth's portrait is dated 1902, a year before she died giving birth to Gloria. She has dark curly hair and strong eyebrows. A "now-face'", as Timo said when he saw it for the first time, adding, "If she was alive today she'd be booked solid, with that Frida Kahlo look of hers".

He glanced at me and I sighed, "Sorry I don't look like her – I have the Cameron genes!"

Elizabeth's gaze follows me down the passage, into my bedroom. I put the suitcase on my bed and walk outside to fetch Timo's large sculpture, which is still in the car. The cow's slow movements, to the left of the labyrinth, remind me to clear the overgrown pathways before the party tonight.

The sculpture rests like a tired toddler against my hip when I walk back up the steps, looking for a level space to put it. Bending down, I notice an opaque white marble that has fallen into a crack in the paving. I had forgotten about my marble games on the front veranda, and how much I had missed this particular one for weeks after its disappearance.

I know it is just a ball of glass, but to me it feels as if it contains the memories of everything I am about to leave forever. I dig it out and clean it, then slip it into the pocket of my jeans.

Excitement rises from my toes and travels upward, making my molars itch from a sudden rush of adrenaline.

Gloria

A box with dark green stripes lies behind a pile of dusty shoes at the bottom of her wardrobe. She fetches it and tips the contents onto the faded quilt, now smoothed over the bed. There are several envelopes, yellowed with age, a small card with mother-of-pearl buttons sewn onto it, and one black and white photograph.

She fans out the envelopes, and with the tip of her index finger outlines Isabel's name with the controlled strokes of a Victorian handwriting. Soft upstrokes and hard down-strokes. Her granddaughter's name is underlined with a generous curving stroke.

Gloria's eyes stray to the photograph and her eyes meet those of her granddaughter: dark pools under the sharp line of her short fringe; timeless eyes that convey the ability to sit quietly and wait. With a shiver, she turns the photo upside down so that Isabel's face is hidden against the quilt.

She picks up one of the envelopes and reads the letter inside.

Dear Isabel,

One cannot throw someone else's shadow. Did you know that? I often dream that I am walking on a dusty road, in the late afternoon, my shadow a long stretch of liquorice in front of me, when I suddenly realise that it is not my shadow at all. It wears a hat, and my head is bare. Its arms are swinging by its side, and mine are folded across my chest. In my dreams I always cast someone else's shadow.

Today I felt like writing a happy letter but already it feels a little sad. Under the weather. What do you think that means? To be under the weather? Under a dark cloud, perhaps. But then I should be happy. I am like you; we like dark clouds and the promise of rain. The smell of moisture in the air.

I have noticed how you flush red and become sweaty at the merest hint of sunshine. Ruth overdresses you, she doesn't understand. The sun asks too much and gives too little.

Animal, vegetable, mineral. This little string of words has been hanging in my head for days. I am animal. I am mineral. Not vegetable, I hope!

See, no need for sunshine after all!

Love,
Your grandma Gloria.

Her hands tremble as she puts the letter back into its envelope. She is reminded of her first silkworms, and how she lifted them out of their box with her hands shaking, to put fresh leaves in. Part of her wanted to hurt them, but she was afraid of the ooze inside their skins. She remembers wondering how much pressure their bodies could take; how hard she would have to squeeze to get them to burst. She never managed to squeeze hard enough, and never found out.

Gloria buries her hands under the pile of unsent letters, stirring the sour smell of stale dust into the room. She wonders, what fool wrote this nonsense?

From her mouth tumble meaningless words, a string of names and places, along with a laugh that startles over her lips. She had written these letters to Isabel a long time ago. 1957. 42 years ago. The number 42 pops into her head. A neat number, she thinks. It was the street number of the first house she and Frankie lived in after they got married. 42 Lewis Road, Worcester. On the edge of town. The mountains of the Valley of

Witches surrounded the town. *Hexriviervallei.*

They moved to Worcester just after their wedding, and lived there until moving back to Muizenberg when Ruth was five years old.

Cold ashes stirred in the fireplace as early morning crawled over the pale grass and greeted her where she sat, knitting socks with thin needles, painful stabbing, always. The wool was a tightrope stretching into the future.

Knitting had become a compulsion, and she carried a basket of wool wherever she went – Patons Moorland Double Knit. With a pair of no. 9 "Beehive" needles she cast the first of the 162 stitches needed to knit a blanket for Ruth. The required tension was six stitches and eight rows to an inch, and while she knitted the test piece she glanced at the words in the pattern book at her feet and attempted a lullaby. Strands of wool slipped through her fingers, threads of colour woven through months of waiting amid the mountains, her index finger soon stabbed raw.

*

The letter safely back in its envelope, Gloria recalls the liquorice shadow on the dusty road, which reminds her of the last evening of Frankie's life. She had visited him in hospital and when it was time for her to leave he struggled out of his bed to give her a hug.

"Body to body," he had said, " Not just cheek to cheek."

The late afternoon sun spilled through the window and pulled their shadows from their bodies, stretching them into two thin lines on the polished linoleum floor.

"I'm fine. I want to be alone," she told Ruth and David, last of the visitors to leave after Frankie's funeral tea.

"Goodbye, Isabel," she added, turning to face her granddaughter. But Isabel tucked her chin to her chest, refusing to meet her grandmother's gaze.

Then Gloria poured herself a drink, not bothering with ice, soda, or water. She savoured the burn on her tongue, then swallowed. And walking outside to the veranda she wiped at her left eye, and looked blindly at the view beyond.

"Laid to rest," she said, raising her glass at the low-tide waves languidly stroking the rocks. Leaning her back against the wooden slats of the bench, she felt utterly alone, a tired old sentry patrolling the blurry edges of her life.

The word *termagant* came into her head. Isabel had once formed that word during Scrabble, a game that they both enjoyed. She was then about seven years old, and very proud of every new word she discovered. Gloria insisted on looking it up in a dictionary, and read it out loud.

"Termagant: Bad-tempered, noisy woman. Name of a heathen deity."

She looked up at Isabel's steady gaze.

"Oh," Isabel had said, "Is that what it means!"

It was her third night without Frankie. She sat outside until the moonless sky wrapped around her eyes, and obliterated the waves and rocks. In a dark corner at the bottom of the garden lay a rotting pile of cardboard boxes that Frankie was meant to take away. But he died instead. She could smell the musty odour of wet rot as they composted back into soil.

She put her glass down on the table and pulled a sheet of paper closer. Frankie's tortoiseshell fountain pen felt large and slippery in her hand as she started to write:

Dear Isabel,
We have to lie to live. The heart bleeds with so much unsaid,

and the liver turns grey with abuse. The night comes as a blessing and draws the blinds on moments lost forever. Bowls are lined up in the morning to break the fast. As the boat goes out in the morning, the rope unfurls behind it, trailing a snailpath in the water. Shut the door and turn the key: Remember, we have to lie to live.

Down the garden path I go.

So many birthday cakes uniced and cold. Folded dresses never worn, and rusty keys that don't turn.

Love,

Gloria, grandmother.

A silverblue earshell lay on the table next to her. She picked it up.

"Happier times, as they say," she whispered into the night.

Gloria put the shell to her ear and listened for an answer. She heard the rushing of her own blood. Vibrating cellular matter. Then looked down at the words under her hand and slipped the folded letter into her shirt pocket.

Sleep was a long time coming as she lay waiting on her back, one arm lifted onto Frankie's cold pillow. She entered the first dream of the night half awake, dancing inside a giant shell, sliding from the top down to the bottom. She kept her eyes on her toes, noticing how they wriggled and squirmed. The mouth of the spiral beckoned and she threw herself with arms wide open into the darkness.

Ruth

The surface of the table is cleared; all the knives and spoons and forks packed away. She sits down at the table and opens her cookbook at a green-flag marker. Her eyes find one of Isabel's favourite recipes, *Risi e Bisi.*

Reading old familiar recipes calms her down: tracing her finger down the list of ingredients that used to be standard stock in her pantry. Butter, olive oil, bacon, shallots, chicken stock, Italian short grain rice, shelled fresh peas, parsley, Parmesan cheese.

Isabel loved shelling peas, but when Ruth brought home some mange-tout peas one day, she refused to eat them.

"It's French for eat-it-all, go ahead, have some," her mother urged, but Isabel refused.

"They're too beautiful to eat," her daughter said, holding a pod up to the light, looking at the swollen pea-bellies showing through the luminous green skin.

She reads the recipe out loud, "Heat butter and oil in a large saucepan and cook bacon and shallots about 5 minutes. Add stock and rice, bring to the boil and stir well."

Her mouth begins to water, and she feels the texture of finely grated Parmesan cheese, sprinkling it over David's plate.

On end-of-term days Isabel always invited Sarie home, and Ruth made Knickerbocker Glories with strawberry syrup for lunch. Isabel called them Knickerbocker Gories because the red syrup ran like blood down the inside of the glasses.

Ruth's father, Frankie, used to paint her nails the colour of strawberry syrup, holding her hand in his, stroking on the colour with a small black brush.

"It tickles!" she giggled, as she tried to pull her hand away.

"Wait," he said, "Hold still, almost done," then blew hot breath onto each nail.

Isabel and Sarie didn't speak while they ate their treat; just grinned at each other over sticky spoons like accomplices who had managed to solve a mystery. Cleaning up in the kitchen, Ruth overheard their conversations, or as Isabel said, *hoverheard*.

"Stop spying on me, Mom, go away," she told her mother, and continued when she was sure Ruth was out of earshot.

*

They seldom ate a large meal on Sundays because Ruth did the week's ironing when David went to church. Isabel would lie on the floor of the kitchen, on an old rug, and pretend to read. She watched as her mother smoothed the wrinkled piles of clothes, she watched as the angry heap of sheets and pillowcases turned into smooth, silent squares. By the time David got back from church, he also seemed ironed out and calm. Ruth kissed him on his cheek and said, "Welcome home."

In summer they had bowls of strawberry coulis to celebrate his return, which Ruth made with fresh strawberries and water and castor sugar.

"Pastor sugar," Isabel said as she pressed a damp finger onto the spilled grains on the table, and winked at her dark-suited father.

Gloria

Moving the letters aside, Gloria gets up from the bed, tightening the belt of her dressing gown. A memory brightens the fog of her calcified arteries.

Holding onto the belt, she tilts her head to the image of a young woman with dark curly hair and watches as she places three bowls on a kitchen table. She smiles at the woman and says "One for Frankie, one for baby Ruth, and one for myself." She mimes the younger woman's movements. Together the women spoon hot oats into the cool whiteness of the bowls, sprinkling a layer of sugar on top. It melts into dark, sweet puddles. They pour the milk over last. Then call out, in a singsong voice, "Breakfast is ready!"

Memories itch across her skin, a fungal growth that cannot be soothed. Her mind is a needle, sewing riddles, and she whispers, "Today-is-yesterday's-tomorrow-and-tomorrow's-yesterday . . . "

Through the window she notices a string of birds, black pearls on an invisible thread that forms an endless pattern into infinity. She strings Scrabble-words together like beads to calm herself, "Eland-dragon-gory-yellow-wedding-gnome . . . " then tightens the belt a little more and smoothes her hair. Turns on her bright face. This feels like a good day, Gloria thinks.

A fresh sea-smell enters through the window of her bedroom, the one that has never closed properly. As a child, she used to sit in front of this window and look at the luminous full-moon path rippling across the water towards her. Worrying about this hole in their house, where the smell of seaweed and fish entered. She knew it would continue to enter even after she was dead and gone.

On hot midsummer nights the smell of rotten *rooiaas* reminded her of the smell of her monthly rags.

Playing in the rock pools outside her house, Gloria watched as greedy fishermen inserted short, sharp knives into the ball-shaped clusters of redbait. Their fingers poked and prodded the slimy orange flesh, scraping the bait free from their hard casings.

Nothing was safe from the prying fingers; the fishermen always got what they wanted.

An open suitcase lies on the floor on Frankie's side of the bed. Gloria sits down on the low stool in front of it, and starts unpacking. She is looking for something to give to Morgan, a gift to take with her to Scotland.

When she and Frankie were forced to move from their home in Worcester, back to the sea-side home her father had left her after his death, she wrapped her blocks of watercolour in her mother's lace handkerchiefs. She placed them, together with rolls of paper and the small wooden easel her father had made for her, into the packing crate.

Whenever her father returned from his coastal salesman travels he brought her gifts of paints; colour samples from the imported art supplies he sold. And brushes and paper. Gifts of words also tumbled from his lips, their opaqueness matching his eyes.

"Tempera . . . chassis . . . casein . . . marouflage." He wrote the words down on scraps of paper and handed them to his daughter with no explanation, then continued to talk about the temperature of colour. He mentioned hot pigeon blood ruby, and the cool blue of wildwood violets. Gloria had never seen a wood before, or violets. Only sea and blue sky and birdwing.

"Sulphur yellow," tumbled out from his mouth one day, and foamspittle formed in the corners of his mouth. *Sulphur* became the yellow of her father's spit.

"Hot, cold, cool, warm," she said as he pointed randomly at his colour chart.

"Paint," he said, "Why don't you? Your mother did, *en jy is jou ma se kind.*" Her father spoke his wife's tongue, Afrikaans, out of respect for the dead.

Gloria didn't want to be her mother with a tongue doubling in size when she tried to speak English, but accepted her father's gifts. She tried to memorise the names of the colours on the charts, turned into rare, polished gemstones by his endless reciting.

"Orpiment, madder, vermilion, malachite green, vert azure, azur allemagne, yellow lake, yellow ochre." He stroked each colour with his thumb before moving to the next one.

"These are the colours that formed the palette of Rubens," he told his daughter, "The powdered pigments are now locked away in a museum where they fade more and more each day . . . the vegetable pigments, the greens, are almost gone."

After her father's death, Gloria decided to paint the pictures he had imagined for her. She used the colours Elizabeth dreamed of while she carried her child, in that space that Gloria had elbowed out between lung and liver and spleen. Colour pulsed through, onto her developing retina, and the nerves of eye and brain. The same colours Patrick had named as if repeating a sacred incantation to resurrect his wife, wishing he could translate them into her mother tongue, Afrikaans.

The eye is the final judge, and it closed on the streaks of paint down Elizabeth's legs, flaking off to reveal the veins visible through her skin. The painting of a kitchen cupboard interrupted because of Gloria's insistence on being born under a full moon.

The stiff, stained parcel of colours is pushed into the corner of the suitcase. Gloria unwraps it, wets a finger, and rubs it onto the red block. Then draws a crimson line on the paper backing of the lid of the open suitcase. Tears wet her cheeks, as if oozing straight through her skin.

"Stop it!" Frankie had shouted, when he found her with her parcelled colours, locking up the empty house in Worcester, crying soundlessly. "Stop all that crying!"

The smell of iron oxide remains on her fingertips as she replaces the red block, the smell of bloodlust, and the colour of her memories. She closes the parcel of colour and puts it on her bed. Cocks her head to the sound of her dead father's voice: "Listen," he says, "Most importantly, if a pigment is not permanent, the other properties need not matter much to an artist, at least not to anyone who is working for anything other than a temporary reputation."

"Listen," he says again, "This is important . . . colour, transparency, opacity, specific gravity, working quality, fineness of texture, body. Those are the physical characteristics of pigment . . . now the chemical: permanence, crispness and setting up, drying power. Do you understand, child? If you don't, it is no use pretending to be an artist, no use."

The second item she lifts from the suitcase is a hand-sewn brassiere, made by her Aunt Johanna, to fit her thirteen-year-old niece.

Gloria's breasts were barely contained in this cloth harness. Red welts chafed onto her skin. These stiff contraptions were made by her aunt to tame the bounce. Her Aunt's upholstered bosom heaved as she breathed through her nose, pins in her mouth. Gloria noticed how breasts became *bosom* at a certain age, the two becoming one.

She slips her arms through the brassiere straps and walks to the oval ebony-rimmed mirror. A naked girl stares back at her. The generous cups are wrinkled and covered with spots of dark green mould. She turns up the volume of her hearing-aid to catch the girl's whisper, "Breasts-of-rage-grubby-fist-in-a-cage . . . "

Reflected in the mirror a white towel lies like a bride's veil around the feet of the girl.

Gloria's legs lift high to step outside its moist circle and she tilts the ebony-rimmed oval back. She sticks out her tongue. It is broad and red, almost purple, and she wonders how other tongues look, not having seen many. The open bedroom door is reflected in the mirror. A broad wooden threshold separates her bedroom from the passage. At thirteen she was careful not to step onto it, fearing the bony-fingered childhood that still lurked would grab her by the ankles.

She always entered the kitchen in the mornings feeling like a harnessed filly, reporting for duty. With tamed breasts in their cloth hammock. She thought of the boys' eyes not meeting hers at school when her breasts became visible. Suddenly, they didn't know where to look.

"Morning Father!" she said, greeting him in the kitchen.

The oatmeal was on the shelf behind him, and she had to squeeze past because he wouldn't move. He coughed a wordless response, he liked the heat of her body and she wanted to choke and scream all at once, pushing into the narrow space. Her father's red-eyed stares crept hotly over her skin. "Shame," the visitors said. "Pity about the child, she grows up the hard way, but she can take it."

The box fell from the shelf one day, as she pushed past her father, and ivory oatmeal flakes tumbled out, settling on his dark green jersey and floating on top of the liquid in his glass. Patrick got up to rinse his glass and Gloria thought of her mother's eyes behind the condensation in the bathroom. He screwed the cap back onto the green bottle.

"Medicine," he said, tapping the bottle with his finger. "Join me sometime, why don't you?"

74

Gloria felt drawn to the liquid in the glass, to her father's eyes, grey caves after the third or fourth glass. Moving to open the tap, she knocked her head on the corner of the pale blue shelf Elizabeth had painted, the last stroke still visible. She sank to her haunches and cried as he spoke to her in her dead mother's tongue.

"*Huil help niks,*" he said, but Gloria told him crying did help, look at him, never a dry eye. She leaned her head against his knees.

"Your mother's hair," he said, lacing his fingers into the dark growth, "You have her hair."

Isabel

I look behind me and notice that the salty moisture has plumped out my footsteps so that they all but disappear.

An invisible hand attempts to erase the memory of my journey.

Liar, liar.

I was ten years old when my grandfather died. The only way I could fall asleep was to suck condensed milk through one of the two holes I made in the top of the tin with one of my mother's sharp kitchen knives.

On the night he died I sucked a mouthful and then kept it on the bowl of my curled-up tongue until saliva diluted it into the consistency of warm, sweet milk. Only then did I swallow it, a warm breast-milk substitute.

From the bathroom across the passage came the strange, unfamiliar smell of my asparagus urine. Earlier that evening I had eaten a whole plate of it, and Ruth had scolded me, "Isabel, no! Not the asparagus! They were for the grown-ups!"

Asparagus speared its pompous sound into the kitchen as I swallowed the last one and apologised.

The first dream of the night was interrupted by the loud ring of the telephone in the passage outside my bedroom. I sat up, listening, the taste of sugar and milk still on my tongue, a furry coating on my teeth.

My mother answered the phone, her voice sleepy. I held my breath and listened to the long silence that followed, finally interrupted by my father's voice. "Who are you talking to?"

Ruth put the phone down and cried. David must have held her, because her crying sounded muffled. It didn't last long.

"Well," she said, "That is that, then. How will Gloria cope, now that he is gone?" My mother and father walked past my bedroom to theirs, closing my door softly.

I started to cry, hugging my knees and rocking back and forth on my bed.

The funeral was held three days later, and afterwards Gloria gave me Frankie's old black suit with coattails and top hat.

"You were his favourite," she said, "I want you to have this."

My father told me about The After-Life. About Eternity Next To Our Father. And that is where I imagined my grandfather to be. Two grey-haired men sitting next to each other, staring into infinite space.

"In order to be saved, one has to be lost," David once told me, trying to explain the principles of sacred geometry, patterned pages scattered on the table where we sat. After my grandfather's funeral, in the moments before sleep, I saw those patterns repeating endlessly, a muddled image repeating over and over and over. Becoming an endless stream of tomato cans rolling into an empty grave.

My father believed in God Almighty but I always knew that my mother didn't, because she had a nose for lies. Rearranging the bookshelves in my father's study one evening, I heard my mother's voice: "David, I'm organising your books into a system of fiction and non-fiction. Where should I put all these books on religion?"

*

I scan the surface of the beach for unusual seeds, always hoping for a rare sea bean from a faraway place.

Jonathan has told me the names of the most commonly found of these trans-oceanic travellers, seeds that are dropped by the wind, and gravity, into tropical rivers and propelled by their currents into the ocean.

Sometimes staying afloat for as long as 30 years.

Screw Pine, Box Fruit, Puzzle Fruit, Sea Heart, Crabwood, Anchovy Pear, Coral Bean.

Years ago I found a photograph of a Screw Pine flower in one of my mother's cookbooks. It was the strangest-looking flower I had ever seen; its inner core of densely packed tiny flowers resembled a teased-out ball of pale cream-coloured silk thread. Ruth uses Screw Pine flower essence when cooking Indian dishes; just a small drop of this fragrant essence is needed to flavour one kilogram of meat.

The Sea Heart is a black heart-shaped seed.

"*Entada gigas,* six centimetres long, from the New World tropics," Jonathan said, as he showed me a photograph. Then pointed to another, "Gingko seeds are incredible. They can wait for three hundred years for the right circumstances and guaranteed germination."

"No wonder Gingko Biloba is prescribed as an antidote to memory loss."

"It's a very good example of an indehiscent seed, hanging on to its genetic cargo until the time is right."

"And what would you call the seeds of that blue-flowered plant at the front door that shoots out its seed on hot days, like firecrackers going off?"

"Dehiscent," he said.

I love the sound of my husband's voice. Its low, warm sound turns everything he says into private, intimate information.

The dark, crooked line left on the beach by last night's high tide brings the word *flotsam* to the surface. Float some. Perfect. Flotsam is a beautiful word for something rather ugly. Scummy, broken residue.

But it is a word that perhaps promises hope.

Many seeds, blown here by the wind, or brought in by the sea's currents, form part of this residue. They have missed their chance to germinate, stranded on barren sand.

Untangling yet another shark egg from a piece of seaweed, I search for the Afrikaans equivalent of *flotsam*. I think of *gemors*, which means rubbish, trash, garbage. But that is not the right word at all.

My father, David Cameron, added weight to the scales that already tipped in favour of English as my first tongue. He was the son of a devout Presbyterian missionary who immigrated to South Africa in 1927. In time, however, the missionary's faith seeped away into the thirsty African soil and his son, David, grew up in the dry riverbed of duty and denial that remained.

When David met Ruth, he was shocked to find someone to whom God was a nice idea, but nothing more. A pie-in-the-sky-god.

"Wouldn't it be nice," my mother suggested after their first meeting, "If God really exists?" Her eyes widened at the impossible thought. The soft gutturals of her Afrikaans accent were reminiscent of the rolling Rs of his father's Scottish tongue. He married Ruth anyway, never one to shy away from a challenge.

"I anticipated a glorious conversion," he told me, "I suppose it was the missionary in me . . . like father, like son."

Years before, Gloria's father had been successful in tuning her ear to both languages, and she grew up fully bilingual. Loved her fathertongue, English, hated Afrikaans. Only when she was drunk did she give in to the earthy tug of mothertongue, rooted as it was in womb-memory. My anglophile grandmother was delighted when Ruth married a real, live Scotsman. She felt that she could at last rid herself of the shame of her dead mother's language. Her *kombuistaal* roots.

"I experienced God as absence, not as presence," my mother told me, "Your grandmother's spiritual practice was weekly sessions with a local fortune teller, her own pack of tarot cards, and secret visits to witch-doctors, as sangomas were called when I was growing up."

"We never went to church," she continued, "God's name was a curse, a word you use when you bump your shin on the sharp metal corner of your bed frame, or burn your hand against the oven element."

Walking the tightrope that stretches between my two languages is only possible by keeping my focus elsewhere and never looking down. I am forever stuck, propped among pillows on my mother's kitchen table, cocking my ears towards two different languages.

Music notes emerge, one by one, from behind Kalk Bay mountain, black birds against the pale sky. They fly their lonely song low over the water. I wonder if my grandmother noticed them when they passed her house on the way to the beach.

Morgan

Timo and I live against a mountain slope in Hout Bay, in a small stone cottage we built, slowly, over two years. Large sandstone and quartzite boulders lie scattered in my back garden like a giant's game of marbles. At the end of each day I press my body against the rough surface of my favourite rock, embracing the stored-up sun energy. I love the feeling of warm stone against my skin. Our garden is private, and Timo and I spend a lot of naked time together in the sun.

My mother chose my name, imagining future beach walks with a sea-warrior child. But the sea leaves me cold. Instead, I accepted the gift that came with my father's surname. Stone.

"When – if – you get married, will you keep your maiden name?" my mother once asked.

"What's this 'maiden name' nonsense?" I wanted to know. "I mean, surely the only choice women have is between their father's name, or their husband's name. Or, if they adopt their mother's 'maiden' name, they're stuck anyway with their grandfather's name. And so it carries on and on. What's this feminist 'choice', anyway?"

My mother called my bluff. "So, what are you going to do? Invent your own surname? Create a new, matrilineal line?"

I capitulated. "No – how can I not accept Dad's name? In any case, doing the work I do, Stone is perfect."

Soon after finding the photographs, my mother paid me a visit on the site of a wall I was building in Constantia – a pretext, I knew, to talk about her find in the magazine that day in my bedroom.

"Can you trust him?" she wanted to know, "How do you

know he isn't going to post the photographs on some porn website or something?"

"Well, first of all, that wasn't porn," I said. My mother likes to imagine the worst; exaggeration is her normal state.

"Of course I trust him. Those photographs are private, my gift to Timo. Besides, I have my own set of photos of him, which, thankfully you'll never find."

"Thank God for that," my mother murmured.

She tried to lift a heavy rock lying at her feet, trying to hide her red cheeks.

"As soon as I can, I want to go to Scotland to look at all the bridges built by Thomas Telford," I told her, to change the subject. She interrupted, "Why? You are not an engineer, for heaven's sake!"

I tried to explain. "Most of his bridges were formed with a foundation of large dressed stones, laid by hand and covered with a layer of smaller, tightly-packed broken stones, and whenever I build a wall, that is what I think of . . . all those hands packing stone upon stone across the ages. The method has hardly changed."

We walked the 100-metre length of the half-built wall, stroking the stone with our fingertips.

"The beauty of a well-built dry wall is its durability, and the fact that even if it should tumble down, or collapse, it can be restored time and time again."

*

I wipe the layer of dust from the kitchen table, then remove the wet newspaper from the bunch of tulips I have brought in from the car. A row of three vases stands on the windowsill. I lean over the sink and place two flowers in each vase. The heat has opened the petals, and I touch the exposed stigma of the single orange tulip. I imagine the pollen tube curling down the style towards the ovule.

Memories of car conversations with my mother intrude.

"A flower needs the following to perform its function . . . gamete producing tissue, which is . . . which are . . . anthers and ovules, petals to protect the reproductive tissue, petals or nectar to attract the pollinators, protection for the seed by the ovary . . . the embryo is nourished by food stored in the seed."

"Just like with real babies."

I rested my finger on the page and pulled away from my mother's hand reaching out to tuck a stray strand of hair behind my ear.

"Not really. We don't have petals and nectar, or anthers . . . and *please* don't ask if anthers are like antlers!"

"We use perfume and pretty clothes to attract a mate . . . "

"Oh puh-lease Mom, I don't do any of that stuff to attract a mate!"

One orange petal is dangling downwards, attached just below the anthers, which are deep velvet purple. I flick my forefinger against it, and a fine dusting of pollen falls onto the windowsill, along with the petal.

I smile and place my hand over my belly.

Isabel

The sandy beach under my feet offers a different habitat to that of rocky shores. Animals living here choose the depth where they find their ideal living conditions. They dig deeper if the sand is hot and dry; migrate upward if oxygen levels fall too low.

Small plough snails emerge from the wet sand and I watch one of them gliding towards the water. It leaves a trail of wrinkled ribbon behind. As it meets the rising tide it turns on its back and uses a large foot as a rudder. The next wave will drop it where it will find food. The presence of the snails' labyrinthine pathways on a beach indicates safe swimming conditions – they cannot survive where there are dangerous rip currents.

Bending down to have a closer look I think of the stone labyrinth that Morgan built in McGregor. She loves dry-walling, stacking stone upon stone without the aid of mortar. Matchmaking; fitting this one's belly into that one's curved back. After David died Morgan and I built a cairn for him using the leftover white stones from the labyrinth paths.

*

When I was thirteen years old I thought of my father's vocal cords as conveyer belts carrying waste from a tired old mine, no sparkly jewels left to uncover. Without noticing, he had turned into his own father. David died three years ago, but I can still hear his voice when I speak. I hear the sad finality of his voice when I arrive at the end of a sentence, almost a sigh.

After supper, as I swallowed my last morsel of finely chewed food, I raced my mother to a sentence. We excluded my father from our after-dinner conversations because he was lost in his own private world. Throughout his meals he spoke softly to himself, gesticulating with his knife, or fork, tapping with the back of his knife on the table to get a point across to whomever it was he was speaking to. This he did while chewing every mouthful twenty times. His silent chewing took him to people and places we knew nothing of.

Sometimes he traced geometric patterns with the tip of his knife onto the white damask tablecloth he insisted on having beneath his plate of food. He taught mathematics at the local university, and since that was not a language I understood, I never found a point of entry into his world.

Unsaid words lay amid the polite scraping of cutlery on porcelain.

Ruth usually itched to clear the table after supper, to restore some order, to get the dishes over and done with. So that she could retreat to her bed with one of the many cookbooks that she devoured daily. Imagining dishes she could prepare for my grandmother, one last meal to force Gloria to want to live. She planned elaborate feasts to tempt her away from all the green bottles holding alcohol, and the brown ones holding pills.

I was never fast enough to escape the table before my father cleared his throat to make way for the Words of God.

"Fetch me the Bible, Isabel," he would say, taking his reading glasses from his shirt pocket. Ruth rolled her eyes and leant her elbows on the table, her fingers woven into a small nest.

David had made the kitchen table after marrying my mother, when they moved into their first home. During its construction he sawed into his left index finger, and the blood seeped into the thirsty mountain pine. It seemed an appropriately dramatic seal to love's labour, and he never tried to remove it. My mother, my father, and I sat at the end closest to the stove, and furthest away from the mark at the other end.

I knew of nests as safe places, but had also learned at school about lairs, the nests of predators. Looking at my mother's hands, I wondered what she was holding prisoner.

My black tyre swing hung from the arm of the oak tree in our garden. Listening to my father's voice I felt its dark shape calling me. He liked to read about regulations regarding infectious skin diseases, purification after childbirth, regulations on mildew, and also about all the many bodily discharges from infectious diseases. The Book of Leviticus provided him with the illusion of being the maker of laws in our home.

Ruth sat quiet and still during David's reading. She hid her godless feelings from me by looking down at her hands.

"Any bed the man with a discharge lies on will be unclean, and anything he sits on will be unclean . . ." Right up to: " . . . the Lord spoke to Moses and Aaron."

Before getting into bed that night, I re-read the passage my father had chosen, his voice a faint echo in the air, thin as the paper supporting God's words. I found that he had skipped a whole lot of verses. In these, the word *semen* was often mentioned.

I sat still and stiff-backed, trapped in the dust of my father's voice. My head tilted to one side in a posture that I hoped conveyed interest and understanding, as I sneaked sideways glances at my split ends. My straight hair was thick and heavy. I preferred it to my mother's candyfloss mop. And even though I had my father's straight nose and his freckles on my cheeks, I suspected that I was adopted.

The God of Leviticus grew ten feet tall as I listened to my father's Old Testament-reading, and I fantasised about having Him on my side. His thundering voice commanded: "Keep all my decrees and laws and follow them, so that the land where I am bringing you to live may not vomit you out!"

My father read about the Day of Atonement, and explained that it was the day of forgiveness. Aaron sacrificed "the bull for his own sin, offering to make atonement for himself and his household."

As he read on and on I saw a child pulling open a drawer, or trying to, but it was stuck fast and would not move. My father's voice continued, "He is to take some of the bull's blood and with his finger sprinkle it on the front of the atonement cover; then he shall sprinkle some of it with his finger seven times before the atonement cover." I saw a pile of pale blue handkerchiefs, stained with speckles of rust. The white tablecloth covered the bloodstain on our table, but I saw it slide across the table towards me. I saw the escaped goats kicking and bucking as Aaron tried to catch them, hearing God's voice commanding: "He is to cast lots for the two goats – one lot for the Lord and the other for the scapegoat. Aaron shall bring the goat whose lot falls to the Lord and sacrifice it for a sin offering. But the goat chosen by lot as the scapegoat shall be presented alive before the Lord to be used for making atonement by sending it into the desert as a scapegoat."

After my father's reading I was expected to recite a verse I had memorised. I listened until he read an easy passage and then repeated it over and over until he stopped reading. Before he could even ask, I blurted it out.

"These are the birds you are to detest and not eat because they are detestable: the eagle, the . . . vulture, the black vulture, the red kite, any kind of kite, any kind of raven, the . . . some kind of owl, the screech owl, the gull . . . hawks, the little owl, the cormorant, another kind of great owl, the white owl, the desert owl, the osprey, the stork, any kind of heron, the hoopoe and the bat. I think I got them all."

"You have to be stark raving mad to want to eat any of those, voluntarily," was Ruth's only offering, her hand already reaching for a cookbook.

Back at school I told Sarie about all the detestable things my father read from the Bible.

"All flying insects that walk on all fours are to be detestable to you," I told her, and she replied, "But you may eat those with jointed legs that hop on the ground . . . thank you very much, God, for your kindness!"

It felt good to be given permission to detest so many things.

"Detest, detest, detest!" we chorused after maths lessons, and "Detest, detest, detest!" we whispered when passing the boy with weeping eczema patches behind his knees.

Gloria

G loria enters the kitchen. She remembers the grit of sea sand brought in as crusty anklets after a foamy walk with her father. Coming home, she would place on the windowsill sea-tumbled bits of glass she had found on the beach. Sometimes, sitting next to him on a rock, she didn't hate him. He pointed, "Cormorant!" to the outstretched wings in silent prayer, or "Tern!" or "Gull!"

Moulting teenager sea gulls landed next to them on the rocks and Gloria felt tender towards them as she fingertipped her pimpled forehead.

And other times she found him at the kitchen table, slumped and defeated, his face a ravished landscape. As he placed his lips against the rim of his glass, she imagined smoothing over the hurt with careful thumbs.

"There, there," she imagined saying, "All better now."

Everything Gloria owns had once belonged to her mother. Death denied Elizabeth these heavy possessions that now stand in her daughter's house.

She opens the tap and washes the red smell from her hands, then sits down at her mother's kitchen table and places the wrapped colours next to her. Her head droops onto her crossed forearms, her thin shoulder blades push against the purple fabric of her dressing gown. In front of her is a pile of green beans. Waiting for Frankie to come home, she used to cut up piles of green beans, releasing their fresh sperm smell into the air.

Every day she would wait for her husband to come home after his busy day.

She lifts her head and picks up a bean, holding it against her shirt. Purple and green. Isabel's favourite colours, she thinks, and takes out a green watercolour block from the parcel next to her.

On the day they moved from Worcester to Cape Town a large green van, *terre verte* canvas, stood outside their Worcester home, waiting. She felt shame, watching the curious neighbours' curtains twitch, held by fingers that pulled them tightly closed as their gaze met hers. She leaned into the blinding green sun, reflected off the side of the van, watching her motherchair disappear into a black hole.

"Careful!" she shouted into the heat.

*

Walking to the bathroom with the block of green in her hand, she hears Patrick's voice, "Listen, child, pigments have physical and chemical properties, here is a list of the physical," and sees his fingers trace the words down the page of his coffee-stained art materials manual, the worse for wear after many travels.

In the bathroom she lifts the seat of the toilet and throws the colour-block into the white enamel throat. A green cloud rises to the surface as she pulls the chain.

Back in her bedroom she lifts a pair of underpants from her mother's chair. It sits straight-backed next to her bed, silently watching over her when she sleeps. She folds the underpants and places them on a shelf in her cupboard. When she was younger the underpants were often stained, despite the wad of rags between her legs. She threw the previous day's dirty rags in a wooden crate from her father's South Coast travels –

it remained hidden at the bottom of her cupboard until the smell seeped into the room. The stained rags were then buried in the garden.

While getting dressed in the mornings she would listen to her father in the kitchen as he clinked glass against bottle in a toast to himself, next to a pile of unwashed dishes in the sink, a feeding trough for cockroaches. Shadows on the wall shifted as the sun broke free from the morning mist. She rolled her eyes at the spiders. "Eight o' clock in the goddamn morning and his glass already empty, who will look after him when I am gone?" She turned around, away from the spiders and reached for the cupboard door. "I don't intend staying around for long, learnt that from her . . . first man I meet I'll marry."

*

Gloria returns to the low stool in front of the suitcase next to her bed, and resumes her unpacking. She hasn't yet found what she is looking for. Another lace handkerchief, a faded blue, is wrapped around a shard of mirror. It lies on top of a cardboard box. One of its sharp points has pushed through the lacework, and pricks her finger as she lifts it out. She sucks the drop of blood away, then traces the tip of the shard over the old scars on her wrists.

"No blood left in this old body," she mumbles as she unwraps the mirror from the lace.

"*Gee my 'n soen,*" her father asked when he found her in her bedroom one evening, kissing this shard of mirror. But she laughed and ran away, escaping his mouth puckered in wet anticipation.

Holding the mirror before her, she can see the open door of her bedroom. A left turn through the door would take her into the passage, which ends at the kitchen. Attached to the kitchen is the small room that Patrick moved into after Elizabeth's death.

"You are a woman now," Gloria's aunt had said when she found her niece crying on the beach, trying to bury her bloodstained underwear. Aunt Johanna talked of the monthly release of disappointed eggs, and Gloria covered her ears with her hands, whispering, "Mother-bother-wet-stuff-smother . . . " to block out the words.

"You are a strange one," Aunt Johanna said, "I think you take after your mother."

Gloria sat on the beach, raking through the wet knots in her hair until her scalp hurt. She pinched the soft blue-white skin inside her elbow.

"I can cry if I want to. Whenever," she told her aunt.

Isabel

A stream of pale yellow blows from my fingers. A billion particles of broken shell and other organic matter pour into the wind from my open hand, like thoughts littering my mind before speech; a broken jumble of sounds.

"We don't swear in this house, Isabel," my mother warned when she overheard me in conversation with friends. I liked to try out the words I heard in my grandmother's house, stretching them out like sticky toffees, until the swearword became a long meaningless sound. I loved the tiny wordscabs I found in Afrikaans: *vrot, sies, voetsek.*

Sometimes, sitting on the kitchen table with my legs dangling down and waiting for her to finish making my school sandwiches, I would also say my grandmother's swearwords very fast, *fk, strnt, knt:* small nasal explosions that angered my mother even more.

She pressed the butter knife down so hard onto the slice of bread that it tore.

"Stop that!" she shouted, "Now see what you made me do!"

My mother was a natural cook and I think she would have preferred pre-setting the oven timer for nine months, and taking me out nicely browned on top, smelling of cinnamon and butter. A gingerbread baby. Instead I was red and screaming, protesting my induced entry into this world.

I have suffered from stage fright ever since.

Even now, at 76, Ruth prefers the quiet hum of her refrigerator and the dark gleam of the granite countertop to an evening out with friends. She is the only person I know who is not irritated by the humming of a fridge.

Once home from the hospital, Ruth placed me in a nest of pillows on the kitchen table and immediately started her pointing and naming. Each day was a fragrant journey, beginning with cinnamon sprinkle over warm oats. Midmorning arrived with a square of sun as it hit the tabletop through the window, announcing the arrival of the berry-smell of rosehip tea. Midday brought oniontears to my eyes as the sharp fumes permeated the air. My eyelids grew heavy with the smell of meat frying in their oily juices, signalling suppertime. And closed on lichen patches of turmeric floating on the surface of the rice-water.

Time drifted by on a cloud of cooking aromas, and the spicy smells of curry and cinnamon seeped into my mother's candyfloss hair, held from her face with an Alice band. Her hands smelled of onion and garlic. When her cooking was done she would sprinkle them with salt, rub them together and rinse them with warm water to remove the smell.

The only interruptions to our routine were the urgent phone calls from Gloria. The house I grew up in was a short walk away from my grandmother's. As my mother hurried to save her, yet again, the pram wheels bounced ke-plak, ke-plak over the sidewalk cracks. To me, the word Gloria meant hurry, hurry. Not well. Sick granny. Trains rattled past, their wheels screeching on the salt-encrusted tracks.

One moment I would be sitting on the table, books and bowls and flour and butter all around me, and then suddenly be scooped up by a mad, angry Ruth.

"Time to go to granny Gloria, Isabel. Granny is sick . . . no, no, keep your hat on!"

I somehow always managed to get the hat-wearing business the wrong way round. To my way of thinking it was too hot to wear a hat outside. It made my head sweaty. Whenever I heard the word *outside*, I reached up to remove my hat, which I loved wearing inside.

Ruth left me strapped in my pram at the entrance of the dark passage that led to Gloria's room. She disappeared into the large open doorway that seemed to swallow her whole. I heard angry sounds as I craned forward to catch a glimpse of my mother.

"Mother! Not again! What am I to do with you!"

Of course, I had no idea at the time that my grandmother was trying to kill herself.

*

I walk one foot in front of the other, stepping over kelp and *rooiaas* and hopping sand flies.

The drama of predator chasing prey unfolds all around me. White-fronted sand plovers feast on the sand flies, eating as many as 300 per hour. Sanderlings employ a more brutal method, by nipping off the mussels' siphons with their beaks.

A few gulls fly overhead, searching for white mussels to drop onto rocks.

Whenever I see a mussel plummeting to its death I think back to the summer day when moth-souls floated down onto the red earth under the pepper tree, and I remember the bloodstained handkerchief in my grandfather's bedside cupboard drawer, next to the wooden box. When I looked inside the box that day, I realised that the Earth was indeed round and spinning, and it threatened to throw me off.

Bacteria-rich spume has blown from the sea onto the beach and I step through it, my coat pocket bulging with mermaid's purses and shells. The puffs of spume slide like hovercraft on the shallow waves, which seem to transform into a satin sheet under which Gloria might sleep. My grandmother sleeps so much, seeking oblivion, perhaps.

I try to imagine her as a young woman, sewing scrolls of bright stitches on black satin. I can see the sewing machine placed on top of a kitchen table, in front of a window with a view of snow-capped mountains in the distance. The chair in front of the table remains empty; my grandmother resists my attempts at placing her there: trying to imagine where she must have sat, stringing stitches together like first-graders' pre-writing patterns, and stitching the names of her family in different colours. Ruth's name was stitched in gold thread, followed by a row of Fs and a row of Gs.

Her sewing samplers hang over the back of a chair in Jonathan's study, revealing the small world of her family when they are unrolled.

Gloria gave these linen-backed samplers to my mother, who gave them to me when she moved to a smaller flat in Kenilworth. Whenever I look at them I have an image of my grandmother crying, a *smartvraat,* grief-glutton. I see a weeping left eye with teartracks down a cheek. Ruth's left eye does that too. So does mine. A matriarchal line of left-eyed weepiness.

When Morgan told me that she was moving to Scotland my left eye immediately started weeping. *Smartvraat,* I thought then, just like Gloria.

The stick of kelp that I drag behind me erases my footsteps on the drier, higher sand. Every day I try to notice something new on this overly familiar beach; something I haven't noticed before. Today my eyes refuse to search; instead, they stay with the familiar, with the comfortable sense of belonging, of having seen and examined all.

A woman with red jogging shoes lifts her hand in greeting. I smile and remember the game I sometimes played with my parents. This game gave me the chance to hint at things I coveted. *Covet.* Sinful, Old Testament word. "Thou shalt not!" But I coveted a lot of things, and a pair of red shoes was one of them.

My father saw red shoes as accessories in a sinful act.

"Listen, it's an easy game . . . all you have to do is finish the sentence starting with the words 'You haven't lived until . . . '"

I gave them some examples to wipe the worried frowns off their faces.

"You haven't lived until you have had hair long enough to wear in a ponytail; you haven't lived until you have worn red shoes. See, it's easy."

After listening to the examples, my mother said, "Oh, I see . . . well . . . you haven't lived until you have eaten Magic Tea-Smoked Crispy Chinese Chicken!"

Her eyes sparkled and her mouth moistened, as if she could taste the words, oozing exotic juices.

While speaking, she absent-mindedly pulled at the red page markers identifying her best recipes; the ones that brought a smile to Gloria's face. She became upset when my careless paging made them tumble out, along with dried-out fish moths.

My father took his time, and often needed an elbow prompt from me.

"You haven't lived until . . . until . . . now let me see . . . "

My mother put her hand on his, and opened her mouth as if to speak for him. He pulled his hand away, shaking his head.

"No, no . . . I'll think of something . . . you haven't lived until you have pissed on your own compost heap. Now what do you have to say about that!"

His smile hammocked from ear to ear.

"David!" Ruth hissed, scolding.

It was strange to think of my father's tongue saying *piss* so soon after saying grace.

Ruth

Ruth opens the yellow cookbook at one of Gloria's favourite recipes: braised tongue with sour cream, which Ruth prepared as a special treat for her mother at the lunch three weeks before.

Chopping one onion, one carrot, one stick of celery, on the round wooden board made by David, she arranged this in a roasting pan around one fresh ox tongue, cooked. Butter and sour cream were then mixed with the tongue juice and poured over.

"Here you go," Jonathan had said as he placed the tray on Gloria's lap. "Specially made just for you."

A few boxes remain unpacked, pushed against the wall of her sitting room. She unpacks them mentally several times a day, but is beginning to wonder if she is ever going to turn this wishful thinking into reality.

It is only 10:30 in the morning. She takes off her shoes and lies down on the couch, flicking on the television screen. An infomercial advertising a diet shake that melts fat away crackles to life. Ruth snorts and changes the channel. A woman's face fills the screen, wet with tears.

"Why didn't you tell me?" she demands to know, tugging at the lapels of her lover's suit, "Do I mean nothing to you?"

David frowned, as she told him of Isabel's accusations. "Why are you telling me this?" She was standing at the sink in their Muizenberg kitchen, the purple light of evening transforming the room into an exotic, richly textured place. She thought back to the time spent in that same kitchen when Isabel was a baby, perched on top of the table like a bird in a nest of pillows. Ruth didn't like holding her baby, and it suited her that her hands were always wet, always floured, with buttery fingertips, or clasping a knife.

He didn't want to hear a word of it, didn't want to listen.

"What is wrong with that child?" he said. "Why do you listen to her? You know how she makes stories up all the time, tell her to get over it. Even if it did happen – and I don't think it did – she should just get over it. He is dead and gone, anyway."

"But what if it's true?"

"Did he ever do anything to you? Surely if what Isabel claims is true, then Frankie must have done something to you too?"

As David said this, Ruth remembered one of her father's birthday parties. She remembered Isabel going into Frankie and Gloria's house, emerging a while later from the kitchen door, and sitting alone under the pepper tree in the garden. Frankie then got up and walked to the house, to fetch more drinks for everybody. Before he left he turned to his daughter, and pointing at Isabel who was drawing patterns in the sand, asked: "What's wrong with her?"

She shrugged off her father's question. "She gets like this sometimes, in a world of her own."

Overfed and undernourished are the words that drift into her mind as she swings her legs down, and shifts into a sitting position on the couch. Cooking smells drowned out her guilt – for wasn't the smell of baking bread the supreme sign of a happy home?

Ruth tries to remember how her conversation with David that day had ended. She accused him of being unsympathetic. At that, he exploded.

"The problem with all the men in this family is that they are far too bloody sympathetic! We all put up with far too much nonsense!"

She was sorting the dirty dishes into three piles: cleanish, dirty, very greasy.

"What do you mean by that?" she asked.

"You never stop digging and tunnelling for the truth, and all I know is that too much tunnelling causes the ground to collapse on top of you. And then you die a suffocating death. Just let it be. I don't want to talk about this again."

Later that night as she got into bed, where they slept back to back in an uneasy truce, she realised that she had never answered his question about her father and herself.

She flicks back to the channel advertising the diet shake and memorises the telephone number to order a month's supply.

*

True, and almost true. Those were Isabel's distinctions. Lies were merely truths that have lost their way somehow. They could become truths, given time and circumstance. Not everyone understood this, her daughter had often told her.

Isabel

My head is tilted to the sky and I close my eyes for a moment. If I should trip and fall, I will be labelled as drunk or possibly very ill. On this narrow strip of suburban beach the early morning regulars pay more heed to each other than they would probably care to admit.

The cloying smell of dead animal flesh taints the salty air I inhale deep into my lungs. It emanates from the boarding house on the south side of the beach, and conjures an image of a calf's tongue, purple and pimpled with raised taste buds, simmering in the blue enamel pot Ruth always used for this purpose. I would sit on the kitchen table, reading out loud from a cookbook while I watched my mother prepare the calf's tongue for Sunday lunch. "Pressed Tongue: 1 fresh, salted or smoked ox (beef) tongue, freshly cooked; sauce of your choice to serve. After trimming and skinning tongue, curl it while still warm. Fresh or salted tongues should be soft to the touch, smoked tongue should be firm but not too hard. Blanch it before cooking if salted – ask the butcher. The boiled tongue is cooked when one of the small bones near the root end can be easily pulled out. Remove remaining bones and trim the root, slit underside of skin and remove – the skin should come off easily if you push your thumbs underneath it to ease edges, then peel off." I closed the book and curled my tongue back as far as it would go, like pickled herring in a glass jar.

My mother sometimes prepared tongue on Sundays, when Frankie and Gloria came to lunch with us, and I tried hard not to think of the tongueless animal heads as I diligently chewed

101

each mouthful. My father carved these tongues, cutting straight across at the thickest part, and then changing direction towards the thin end to carve diagonal slices. Watching him, I felt the knife against my own tongue and rolled it into a curled leaf inside my mouth. I nudged him with my elbow, and quoted, "You may eat any animal that has a split hoof completely divided and that chews the cud . . . are you sure this animal's hooves are completely divided and split?"

"Isabel, we are not Jewish. We can eat whatever we like."

There was no direct path to my father's heart. Watching him carve the Sunday meat I attempted small conversations but felt blocked at every turn by God, mathematics, Ruth. I ended up never telling him anything, fearing his frown, his displeasure.

Tongues don't know the meaning of the words they are saying.

My own tongue holds the one memory my mother denies. Filling me up with words without meaning.

No meaning, no feeling.

Teeth keep guard against the bitter tip of my tongue, sweet in the centre and salty down the sides where saliva escapes and trickles back into my throat. How much of my mother tongue do I swallow daily? Dissolved in spit as I speak my father's tongue. Yet I long for my words to float free. Until then I can only find myself outside the hot scrutiny of my mother's tongue.

Curling tongue around tongue I chewed each mouthful at my mother's table twenty times. And swallowed every morsel.

Morgan

I walk outside to fetch a spade and fork from the toolshed. I am wearing my grandfather's felt hat that has his smell. Mostly sweat from "an honest day's work" as he would say, but mixed with the sweet smell of the cigars he occasionally smoked. Timo had brought the cigars with him when he visited my grandfather and me during the time of our labyrinth building.

"You got yourself a good one, Moggie," my grandfather said, nodding his head in Timo's direction while lighting his cigar. Ever since my grandfather helped me rescue the feral kitten I had found in the shed on the farm he called me that. I named the cat Dog – to annoy my mother.

I tried to co-opt my grandfather as an ally against her, to act as a go-between to get her to understand Timo's approach to his work.

"He can't make money doing art photography and making sculptures," I explained. "He coils his pots, and they take forever to make. That's why he got into fashion photography, there is a lot of money to be made if you have what it takes."

"And does he?"

"Yes, he's getting more and more work, the fashion editors really love him!"

"It's strange to hear you talk with so much passion about one of your pet hates, Moggie. Fashion! I never thought I would hear you defend that industry."

"Don't you get it, Grandpa? Timo is using fashion to create art."

"So why is your mother getting her knickers in a knot over it, if it's that simple?"

"She says his photographs encourage violence against women. Invite it, even."

My grandfather coughed, waved the smoke from his face.

"Well, your mother has always had a bee in her bonnet over abuse and that kind of thing."

"Don't get me wrong, I agree with her in principle, but we're talking about fashion photography here!"

Grandpa David asked me to show him an example of Timo's work, and I went inside to fetch the Valentine's issue of *Ma/Donna*.

"What does this funny name mean?" he asked.

"It's a new African fashion magazine celebrating the sacredness of women, all women, mothers, daughters, grandmothers, the lot. Ma, mother, Ma-donna, get it?"

He paged through it while I stood behind him, also looking. The photographs were styled to look like famous paintings and were beautifully lit, using a minimum amount of light.

The first one was based on Auguste Renoir's *Le Moulin de la Galette*. In the bottom right-hand corner a male model leant back against a slatted wooden chair. He was posed talking to two women; the one closest to him draped her arm over the back of a bench. Her eyes were rimmed with red make-up, and purple eye shadow was dusted onto her cheekbones. Her friend leant into their conversation, her right hand on the other woman's right shoulder. They formed a triangle of light in an otherwise dark picture. The dancing couples in the background were barely visible, except for one on the left of the photograph. The clothes they were modelling were gypsy-chic, a layered texture of net, taffeta, silk brocade, velvet. The dress of the woman leaning in was torn from her shoulder. My focus shifted to the dancing couple on the left, and I saw that the model's hand was pulling the velvet skirt away from a bruised and bleeding knee, her eyes also red-rimmed as if she had been crying.

On the facing page, another model was displayed on a large four-poster bed. She had purple bruises under her downcast eyes. My grandfather turned the page; that model's hair was a carefully constructed nest woven with twigs and feathers. Her clothes looked torn.

He closed the magazine and passed it to me. "Your mother may have a point," he said, "and I'm no feminist."

"How can he do this kind of work?" my mother asked when she saw it for the first time.

"These are rape scenes," she said, "with the clothes ripped from the women! And is this a bootprint on the model's face?"

"No, they're patterns," I protested, "And the clothes are designed to look like that."

Timo walked in and Isabel turned to him, "Where do you get your inspiration from? The domestic violence files of the police? Photographs of gang victims?"

"Mom, you always tell me that sarcasm is the lowest form of wit!"

"Well, I have to stoop this low to make it clear how I feel."

Timo stepped forward and took the magazine from Isabel.

"Mrs Stone, I don't think up the look for these models, I don't design or do the make-up, I just light it the best way I can according to the brief of the fashion editors, and shoot."

"I rest my case," my mother said, and walked away. Then turned around and added, "And have a closer look, Morgan, those aren't just pretty patterns, those patterns are designed to look like someone stood on that woman's face."

Gloria

Gloria's lap is filled with balls of red wool, unpacked from the suitcase. Through the window she notices early autumn leaves on a neighbour's grapevine. Some of them are deep red. Before death floats them to the ground, the green disappears and they scream the colour of life.

Every morning as Gloria rubs gritty sleep from the inside corners of her eyes, she hears her father's voice. He always woke her up when he returned home from his coastal travelling salesman trips, even if it was the middle of the night.

"Mastic of tears," he once told her, "is a mysterious compound, formed by the weeping sap of a tree. It is made into varnish to protect paintings." He poured some of the pale yellow crystals into her hand.

She watches the reflection of sunlight and cloud tease ripples of colour on the surface of the moving water outside her open window.

"The human eye can distinguish eighty thousand different tones of colour, do you believe me, child?" Patrick mused, with his colour charts open on his knee.

"Where do all the names come from?" she wanted to know.

"You do not have to name something for it to exist," he said, and she believed him.

Gloria pulls a sheet of paper from the bottom of the suitcase. It is a faded pencil drawing made by Ruth. Of a flower, drawn in a generic way, a kind of follow-the-dots. Ruth had brought this home after her first day at school, and, tracing the contours of the faded flower, she hears her daughter's little-girl voice, "Don't cry, Mommy."

These words had woken Gloria one long-ago morning, when she saw the face of her child and the last dregs of a dream drained away. Early morning light brightened the curtains, and another day began. A day like any other, with dreams turning to dust, until Gloria remembered that it was Ruth's first day at school.

They had been back in her childhood seaside home for a month. Frankie was an inaccessible lump next to her, a hot presence under the blankets. After their move to Muizenberg Gloria's tongue became a lethal weapon, using him as target practice, and not a day passed without her hitting a bull's-eye.

"Witch-bitch!" he shot back when she was sure to hear him.

There would be new people to meet, she thought, a headmaster, and other parents. It was time to put on her face.

The skin over her cheeks felt dry and tight as she rolled away from Frankie, swinging her legs to the carpeted floor. She drained the glass of water next to her bed in one long gulp, and walked slowly to the bathroom where her face waited for her in the mirror above the basin. Pools of purple showed beneath the dry parchment under her eyes, sliding over her cheekbones. She splashed her face, then rubbed a damp cloth under her arms and over the back of her neck.

Using one of her old paintbrushes, she dusted her cheeks with powder, bringing to the surface memories of paint and pencils and the sourbreath smell of brown paper tape sticking damp watercolour paper onto brown boards. Memories of drawing and painting under the tree in the garden of their Worcester home.

She brushed her teeth. Ruth was reflected in the mirror, standing behind her mother. Her eyes filled with tears, and love sparked along this saline current between them. Gloria bent down and held onto Ruth's shoulders.

"I'm scared," her daughter said, looking into her mother's eyes, "What if everybody hates me?"

"But Mommy loves you, darling. You know that, don't you?"

Ruth's eyes looked away from her pleading eyes, and strayed to her mother's lipstick-bleeding mouth. Her hand reached out to touch a long bristly hair sprouting from her mother's chin. Gloria slapped her hand away.

"No! Don't do that! I've told you not to!"

Ruth's eyes filled with more tears, and Gloria turned away from the hot scrutiny of childlove, taking her breath away.

The shadows of her face remained in the mirror as she clasped her hand around that of her child, and walked to school. As they crossed the street to enter the school building, Ruth looked up at Gloria, and said, "Your neck is a different colour than your face, Mommy." Gloria let go of Ruth's hand and breathed out a sigh. "It is not polite to say . . . you're hurting Mommy's feelings."

She left Ruth with Mrs Drabble, the headmistress. Gloria had noticed a thin neck rising from the scooped cloth of her collar. Arum Lily, or Cape Cobra: only time would tell. "You can go home now," Mrs Drabble smiled, as she took Ruth's hand. "Leave her with me."

Walking home, away from her daughter, she remembered the game she used to play with Patrick. They would go outside into the piercing sunlight on the beach, father and daughter, and place a square of green felt on a white sheet of paper. He would tell her about hue, value, chroma, and then lifted the green square after a few minutes of screwed-eyed staring. Together they laughed at the red that hovered blurry-edged in its place.

"Our eyes get tired of seeing the same thing," he explained, "They want to replace it with something else, complementary colour, do you understand, child?"

Isabel

On Saturday mornings my father was disguised as a lawn-god. With his new lawnmower he sent up sprays of fresh green that released the smell of watermelon and cucumber. Every Saturday he clipped his lawn into submission.

He mowed with missionary zeal, invading the territory of the unconverted which, in our suburban existence, translated into a war with weeds. It was my mother who turned mowing the lawn into a religious argument, using words that were as sharp as any knife from the gleaming arsenal she kept in her kitchen, stainless steel blades stuck against the broad magnet screwed to the wall.

"A weed is merely a plant you don't want in *your* garden." Ruth sneered.

I listened as my mother told my father that his obsession with a neatly clipped lawn was a sign of religious fervour. The word *fervour* floated thin-lipped through the gnat-shimmering air to where I lay reading in my black tyre swing. *Fervour* was similar to *flavour,* I decided, but with more bite.

Ruth mocked David's back bent over the lawnmower, "Show me somebody's lawn, and I'll tell you about the state of their soul. A lawn filled with weeds and happy trails of dog-piss is the lawn of a happy soul. Contentment needs no artificial fertilisers."

Ever since my father had used the word *piss* in front of me, it seemed like a perfectly ordinary word, and I began hearing my parents use it all the time. David under his breath: "Oh, piss off." Aimed at my mother. It was the only swearword he allowed to pass over his lips, a rationed portion of mean-spiritedness, a stray weed sprouting from his cropped lawn.

I discovered that you can't piss off in Afrikaans, and started translating the long silences that hung between my parents once the sharp words had blunted the gleam in Ruth's eye.

My father wanted Ruth to be less of something. Ruth-less is ruthless, which is not what he wanted. Just Ruth minus herself.

My mother wanted David to be more.

I saw it most clearly on those Saturday mornings when the sprays of green shot up from the lawnmower, and Ruth stood watching from inside the house.

The tension of unsaid words lay like coiled traps in the shorn lawn, and I escaped to my friend Sarie's house next door.

Morgan

I start building my lunchtime fire the way my grandfather taught me.

"There are only two things to remember when you make a fire," David told me, "Heat rises, and fire needs oxygen, just like us."

Dry wood is plentiful on the farm and after a short walk I have collected enough to start several fires. I place some balled-up newspaper on the ground, covering it with a layer of thin dry twigs. Over this I place five thicker pieces of apricot branch; last season's prunings. Then add the final two logs. I strike a match and place it under the newspaper. It is a matter of personal pride to use only one match to start my fire.

My grandfather's lesson flares into action. A thick tongue of flame leaps through the newspaper, drawn upwards by an invisible force. The twigs catch alight, and soon after, an apricot branch burns too.

The old fire-stick I carved years ago, sitting next to my grandfather, leans against the wall of the fireplace. This is a three-walled enclosure, built on the spot, with loose bricks. It is assembled to perfection every time we cook outside, raising or lowering the walls, as the need arises.

Both of us had a sharp penknife in our hands, whittling away wordlessly, during the month he spent here. I have the same wordless relationship with my father, an easy way of being silent together, because we know each other well.

Waving smoke from my face, I can see my father, with his back turned to me. It is a memory of 1987. I was seventeen, and was visiting him for the first time at his office, on my own. Not

111

one step behind mother, hanging back, the way I used to when I was younger. He was scanning the mountain backdrop outside his office, looking past Rhodes Memorial to the topmost ridge of Table Mountain. I had made an appointment to meet him there for a run up the mountain, through Newlands forest. I liked running alongside my father, too out of breath to talk. We didn't need words, anyway; our skins seemed to communicate as if through osmosis, all our emotions transferred wordlessly.

Unlike the heavy silences that have developed recently between my mother and myself, squashed awkwardly between us. When we hug, it feels as if airbags of safety are released on impact.

Through the clearing mist I can see the church tower in the town of McGregor, lying in the valley below the farm. I fetch the fire stick and lift a collapsed log that threatens to suffocate my fire.

You die when your time's up. The words spark through the hot coals and settle in my thoughts.

When I told my parents of my decision to move to Scotland my mother's reaction was predictably melodramatic.

"We could *die* before we ever see you again!"

"Oh please . . . ! I could get flattened by a bus tomorrow . . . besides, you die when your time's up, Mom."

My mother took her hairband from her hair and wound it around her wrist. She pushed her fingers through her hair, messing it up.

"And Timo?" she asked, "Is he going as well?"

"I don't know, he might. It's not decided."

Actually it was, but I saw no need to tell my mother everything she wanted to know.

My father stood to one side with his arms crossed over his chest. He walked over to Isabel, and put his arm around her shoulders.

This is the image that overlays the earlier one I have of him, scanning the mountain as if to memorise the easiest escape route.

Mother and father, father as protector, his arm around my mother's shoulder. A pre-grader's drawing of "My Parents". As in the photograph of the two of them that my father carries in his wallet. My mother copied a poem by some Afrikaans writer, whose work she is translating, onto the back of it.

Emotional, sentimental proof of their love. Right up Isabel's alley.

I hunch down to make a nest for my lunch among the hot coals.

"We'll miss you . . . of course," my father said, "But we are so happy for you, and proud . . . aren't we Isabel?" His arm squeezed a response from my mother. She attempted a smile.

"Of course . . . you must go, what a fantastic opportunity!"

My mother used to play a game she called "Bartholomew, Bartholomew" on her childhood swing, made from an old car tyre. She told me she imagined herself to be the great explorer Bartolomeu Diaz, braving the high open seas. Kicking her feet higher and higher, she imagined swinging into the blue unknown.

The last time we all had lunch together at Ruth's large house I saw my mother's swing still hanging from the branch of the old oak tree, dangling from frayed ropes. I walked outside and gave it a nudge with my knee as it slid towards me, then stood watching as it swayed in the breeze. Timo joined me, surprising me with a kiss.

"What are you doing out here?" he asked, "Come inside, lunch is ready."

"My mother irritates me so much," I said, looking at the swing.

I could see her, curled into its lap-like space, knees drawn up, dark red hair flying. Those ropes were the last tangible links to her childhood. I grabbed with both hands and swung the empty boat high; on its return journey the ropes shuddered, and snapped.

*

I place the tin foil-wrapped butternut on the glowing coals. It is stuffed with onion and red pepper, and though it looked appetising on the shelf in Woolworths, the thought of it now makes me gag.

What I need is something less rich and wholesome, something that doesn't remind me of my mother.

I need junk food.

Isabel

A large container ship appears on the horizon, seeking shelter in the safe waters of False Bay, as storm clouds continue to darken the sky.

Every time it rains I worry about Morgan, a woman now, who has been driving her own car for almost ten years. I can still see her strapped into the blue safety seat in the back of the car that we bought after she was born. It was a red car and the colour made me nervous.

"A bright colour is safer," Jonathan said when he gave me the keys.

As a child I had stood on the back seat of Ruth's car, as we drove into town and passed shops with patterns painted on their walls. At first, I did not realise that the patterns were words. Until one of them made my mouth move and a sound came out.

"Wall's Ice-cream."

"Where?" Ruth said absentmindedly, and then with excitement, "Isabel! You can read!"

She had tears of happiness in her eyes, and when we got home she sat me down on the table with a cookbook on my lap and told me to read. She cooked and talked at the same time, gesturing wildly with knife in hand. Sometimes it was a spoon, but the flashing of a knife is remembered more easily.

Kitchenwords were added to my world, a world that expanded to contain mother holding a knife in her hands, blisterburns from chillies, Sarie and Knickerbocker Gories, podding the peas. I practised reading the words that belonged to the pictures I knew well. After reading a word I closed my eyes to summon the smell. I was amazed at the tiny insignificance of the word *cumin*. It didn't look like its smell at all.

The idea of sifting flour into a yellow bowl, measuring milk in a see-through jug, or weighing pats of butter, never appealed to me. I didn't want to help Ruth with her cooking, and was happy instead to listen and to read and to smell.

Back when we still had Sunday lunch together as a family, and my father was alive and still lived with my mother, Ruth sometimes spoke Afrikaans to me. She did this mostly to irritate Gloria, who hated hearing "that language," as she described it. Elizabeth's language was passed down the generations like her uncomfortably large pale blue kitchen dresser that ended up in the McGregor house, out of everybody's way.

Moved by her grandfather Patrick's attempts to keep his dead wife's language alive, Ruth decided to speak it often, even though she had never known him. She hung a painted portrait of him in our kitchen and glanced at it when she translated the names of spices, fruits and vegetables, naming and translating simultaneously so that they formed one sound, one word, to my young ears.

"Cinnamonkaneel . . . Saltsout . . . Sugarsuiker . . . Butterbotter . . . Tumericborrie."

Morgan and I still talk of *butterbotter*. Simply because it sounds richer and more satisfying.

Fudge remained fudge, a sticky square of a word oozing between my fingers. The smell of fudge made spit spurt in my mouth. Fudge was a smile on my mother's face.

I told Sarie about the time Ruth took me to the emergency ward at the hospital, tongue-blistered and screaming.

"The one next to the mountain where the wild animals growl all night long."

116

"Chillies down my spine," Sarie said, "I get chillies down my spine, just listening to you . . . you have such an amazing life."

Liar, liar, pants on fire.

Gloria

G loria entered the kitchen one morning, returning from a beach walk with her coat pockets bulging with shells and stones to show her father. She found him dead at the kitchen table. He had drowned in a pool of vomit. She took all the stones and shells from her pockets and placed them next to her father's head, forming a halo.

Then ran to fetch Aunt Johanna, who made all the funeral arrangements while Gloria lay on her bed, staring at the ceiling.

A young man approached her at the funeral.

"Frankie Moss," he said, shaking her hand.

"Pleased to meet you," she replied, noticing the brightness of his eyes, so different to the dark caves of her father's eyes.

Frankie had been in love with Gloria for a while, circling her house like a vulture, keeping his eye on her. Waiting for disaster to strike. Their courtship lasted a month, and ended in marriage. Flattered, Gloria suddenly found herself waking up each morning next to his sleeping form, the wife of this balding man with womanly hips and long thigh bones.

They moved from the house that her father had left her in his will, leaving Aunt Johanna in charge.

"We'll be back," Gloria told her, "The job Frankie got in Worcester is a good one, and I need a change."

"What do you do all day long?" she asked her husband when he returned home from Wolhuter & Sons, the department store where he worked. He smiled, passing her small gifts of buttons, wool, knitting patterns.

"An accountant's job is never done," he said. "There is always something that doesn't quite add up and then we have to start all over again."

Gloria lifts a card filled with mother-of-pearl buttons from the suitcase on the floor, and gets up to fetch the one she found inside the box among the letters. She puts them aside as a possible gift for Morgan.

Three weeks ago at the lunch at Ruth's house, she had seen Morgan and Timo kissing each other next to Isabel's old tyre swing in the garden. She remembered a long-ago night of stars, all the more because of a dark moon, when Ruth was conceived.

Frankie had wrapped her eyes with a length of crepe bandage and steadied her as she stepped over the crumbling weed-choked stone wall that separated their garden from the field beyond. He carried her father's knee rug; all the vomit washed out. They placed the rug on the ground and she straddled her husband roughly; no kitten play or softness, kneading his pale upper body with her fingers. She impaled him on sharp green bottle glass, saliva spurting in her mouth as she cried out, slipping into an endless tunnel where a thousand moths rushed towards her. Pleasure and pain were well-known familiars, like velvet worn thin because of too much wear. And tear.

Frankie's genetic cargo swam through the slippery birth canal and into the wall of womb, muscles gently ebbing into heartbeat, breath. Mothlove and childsoul embraced in greeting, a bundle of cells attached to Gloria's uterine lining.

A zygote became embryo. Once the germ layers had been formed the fate of the cells were determined. A soul arrived to claim it, triggering the expression of the genes. Delicate growths, fingers of *chorionic villi*, protruded from the embryo, into pools of maternal blood, absorbing oxygen and nourishment. On the eighteenth day after conception, Ruth's heart started beating. Blood cells started to form in blood vessels, buds of arms and legs appeared.

*

Gloria strokes the buttons with the tip of a finger; notices a rough spot on one of the knuckles of her right hand. She picks at the soft scab. Droplets of dark red appear on her skin.

Ruth

There is enough time to bake a loaf or two of bread for Morgan, she thinks. Why must she always do as she is told? Morgan is her grandchild and if she wants to bake her a loaf of bread Isabel has no business stopping her.

She walks to one of the boxes pushed against the sitting room wall and pulls it towards the kitchen, hoping to find her bread tins inside. If she dies today, she doesn't want to leave a mess for Isabel to deal with. The box contains a jumble of items, a last pile of sentimental belongings she simply couldn't throw away a month ago when she started packing for the move.

"This is your last chance, Mom," Isabel had cautioned, "Be bold and brave, chuck out all the stuff you don't need anymore."

How do you define need she had thought then, and thinks now, again, as she lifts out the first item, a rusted tin with embossed red roses on the round lid. She twists it off and takes out a crocheted baby bootie, lying next to a taken-apart watch.

"Why aren't there more of us?" Isabel asked Ruth when she came home one day after visiting a friend with four brothers and one sister.

"Well, I did try," Ruth said, and told Isabel about Davey, her older brother. Older, stillborn, dead.

"My brother," Isabel tried out the words, trying to make sense of the muddle of an older brother that never grew bigger than the size of her baby doll. Isabel was older than he would ever be, but he was first.

Ruth fetches a large plastic bag from behind her kitchen door and throws the white bootie into it. She adds the rest of the contents of the rusted tin: the remains of two watches, blind, mute. Disembowelled and broken, they form a pile of small screws and cogs, two numbered faces, four hands, a few springs. David loved taking mechanical things apart but was never any good at reassembling them.

Four white glazed porridge bowls, with chipped rims the colour of bone, smash inside the bag. A Spanish doll with an extravagant black hairdo follows the bowls into the bag. Her dress is torn and dusty. She was a gift from David after an overseas trip.

An LP recording of fairy tales, translated into Afrikaans and read by legendary radio personality, Esmé Euvrard, stands against the inside wall of the box. The story of *Rooikappie* was Isabel's favourite because she liked the drawing of a red-cloaked blonde girl on the cover of the record.

"Can you make me a cloak like that?" her daughter asked, soon after her strange request for a foam rubber chair that had to be shaped like the word *such*.

"No, red doesn't suit you," Ruth said, "Not with your dark red hair."

"Oh well," Ruth says as she snaps the LP record in two. "You told me to be bold and brave." She throws the black shards into the bag and, without looking at the remaining items, takes out and throws away the entire contents of the box until only her collection of kitchen scales remain, wrapped in newsprint, at the bottom of the box. She unwraps them and places them on the table. Three white ones, one light blue, and the pale green one she inherited from Gloria.

Her eyes are streaming from the dust, and she walks to the bathroom to blow her nose and wash her face. She passes her bedroom door and notices the unmade bed. She hasn't made it for a week; just gets out in the morning, back in at night. Nobody's business but mine, she thinks.

Isabel

The air-dried ribbons of white seaweed at my feet remind me of the meal of Spicy Wontons my mother made one night, when I was in Grade Two.

"Prepare yourselves for a real supper surprise!" she announced, arriving home from the Chinese supermarket in town where she had discovered mysterious ingredients.

"I am going to make you Spicy Wontons," Ruth had said with a flutter of her hand, scooping up air, as if it was a vital ingredient in the recipe. Her lips were moist with anticipation and her eyes sparkled – as they always did at the prospect of making a new recipe.

She disappeared into the kitchen and I ran to look up this new word as I heard it – *wanton* – in my brand-new school dictionary.

"Wanton: reckless, heartless or malicious." It confirmed my worst suspicions about my mother. First there was the episode with the chillies and then, when I peered around the kitchen door, I had seen Ruth decapitating a bunch of carrots with one mighty chop.

I wonder if my father knew, as he ate his meal of Spicy Wontons, that he would one day leave his wife, to be closer to God.

The following day I told Sarie that we had vegetables wrapped in the skins of dead baby starlings for supper. It took me a long time to choose the bird; it had to sound just right.

There was a difference between a dead budgie, a dead pigeon and a dead starling.

Starling had just the right sound, slightly forlorn and sad, a fallen star. A dead starling was a sadder thought than a dead pigeon. The smear of red brown on their wings, as if dipped in chocolate, glistened in the sun as they lifted off into the sky. I knew that they mated for life, which made the death of one even more tragic.

*

I untangle the tendrils of the largest mermaid's purse I picked up at the start of my walk, and walk ankle-deep into the water to rinse it, searching for the Afrikaans word. *Meerminbeursie? Haai-eier?* Instead two words for flotsam drift into my head. *Seedrif,* and *wrakhout.* Two beautiful words that speak of drama on the high seas, of ships smashed by brutal waves in a fit of passion. *Drif. Drifsel.*

I always find the right words when I am not searching.

The sun catches the side of the mountain and a broad band of light shoots out like a warning, or a blessing. A Second Coming Jesus-sun.

My shoes dangle from their tied laces, like a basket. Sometimes I hide them in the dense dune bushes at the entrance where I put them on after my walk. I always return from my beach walks with my pockets stuffed with objects. Seeds and mermaids' purses, and clumps of unhappy mating between shark egg tendrils and filigreed seaweed.

Norfolk Pine seeds are blown onto the beach by the wind. They are soft and spongy and strangely female in nature. Bending down, I choose a plump one for Jonathan, even though these seeds are as common as dirt. Not at all like the exotic seeds people send him from all over the country. Jonathan the Seedman.

Before I learnt how to write I drew patterns in the spilled flour on my mother's kitchen table. I smoothed it out first, to make a blank page. With my fingertip I traced what I felt inside.

"Don't you want some paper?" Ruth asked, but I refused her offer. I didn't want my mother to take my drawing from me, and stick it on the wall as Sarie's mother did with hers. I often drew four spiky triangles, forming a wheel with the pointy bits fanning outwards. The bases touched and make a square shape inside. In between the triangles I drew straight lines, longer than the triangle points. I wanted those lines to reach beyond and diminish the mean-looking triangles. On top of the straight lines I put tiny circles, drawn with calming circular movements; round and round.

"Are you drawing a snowflake?" Ruth asked, and I remember feeling amazed that she didn't recognise herself as one of those sharp points with her back turned to the others.

I bend down and draw a simple cross in the wet sand with the piece of kelp I have been trailing behind me. Trapping moisture, this fine beach sand suffers from stagnation, unlike coarse sand, which cannot hold water. My drawing exposes the black, oxygen-deprived sediment that has developed underneath the surface layers.

Like a good witch invoking the spirits, I walk from point to point, touching each one lightly with the wand of kelp. My hair is blowing in the wind, the grey strands exposed.

A curious Black Labrador moves closer and sits down to watch as I point at each name: "Ruth. David. Frankie. Gloria." I have made my peace with the dead. But Ruth and Gloria are still alive.

Reaching the wall separating the beach from the train tracks, I decide to walk one more length before going home, and so, turning around, I walk towards the mountain flank, glittering with clusters of gold where the morning sun catches the windows of the mountainside homes.

A strong wind leans into my back and parts my hair against my scalp. I weave my fingers into my hair, and pull it back from my face. Jonathan likes to do that before he kisses me, and I remember the first time I visited him at his home, soon after we had met. We were walking through his garden, and he stopped at a flowering protea shrub.

"This is the *Protea nitida*," he said, "I think of you whenever I look at it." He spread his fingers through my hair. I remember my reply, although I wasn't sure what he meant.

"It must be its slightly tousled, *deurmekaar* look."

"No, it's not that. It is a wonderfully useful and versatile plant. You can make ink from the leaves, medicine from its bark, and wagon wheels from the wood. And it is beautiful. You should feel honoured."

I gave him a kick on the shin for that unromantic description.

That evening I had supper at his home, and he took out a notebook of diagrams he had made; trying to define me in botanical terms. The questions he had asked himself were whether my leaf shape was linear, ovate, elliptic or oblong? Leaf margin, smooth, toothed, serrated or scalloped? Ovary position? Inferior or superior?

"Plants have the best sex lives," he said.

He traced a line on my collarbone with his finger, before kissing me. I was in love. If he thought I looked like a protea bush, I was willing to accept it.

Last week I wrote Thérèse Bartman's poem, *bewys,* on the back of a photograph he carries in his wallet. It shows the two of us with our arms around each other, squinting at the sun, smiling at our daughter, who took the picture during a summer holiday.

"You'll have to translate," he said. "You know my Afrikaans is pretty poor."

"It tells of a very simple moment, captured by the camera. Proof of the love between two people. *Bewys* means proof. Listen carefully, I'm sure you'll understand it."

Turning the photograph over I read: *"'n oomblik skep gestel/en ons met ons arms om mekaar/die fokuspunt daarin/jou oopknoophemp is blou katoen/jou nek bedwelmd suurlemoen."*

I turned away as Jonathan tried to lick the side of my neck. "Wait," I said, wiping the warm breath from my neck. "Don't do that – anyway, you seem to understand the words very well."

Jonathan took the photograph from me and placed it in his wallet. "I understand more than the words of the poem, Isabel, question is, do you? When are you going to deal with this . . . this *thing*, once and for all?"

At the door I briefly stopped, hearing him sigh. I wished I had an answer to give him.

"Bedwelmd suurlemoen," he said, adding, "And I love you."

I walked out and closed the door behind me.

I give myself over to the rhythm of one foot in front of the other as I turn around for the final lap. The sea is on my left, and I lean into the wind with arms outstretched like a *voëlverskrikker* amongst the sea gulls. My shirt blows tight against menopausal womb-belly. *Ma-boep.*

The last two lines of the poem echo in my head. *Van jou en my die paradys/hou ek die 3 x 5 bewys.* I hold the 3 x 5 proof of you and me and paradise.

As I walk over the dunes and back home again, I pick up a shell. One half of a large bivalve mollusc. It is worn thin and smooth after its long journey. The inside surface is grey-mottled, a lunar landscape. I inhale its smell, and it travels deep, my brain deciphering it as primitive, ancient. Burnt calcium. A forgotten memory. My heart beats a little faster. Smell, I know, is the only sense organ that connects directly with our limbic brain, that part that accesses our primitive past, that warns us of danger.

I put the shell into my coat pocket, reminding myself that nothing is real unless you imagine it to be so.

A woman is walking in front of me, also on her way home. She is my neighbour, but we have never spoken. She releases her ponytail from its rubber band, pulling it again and again through the O of index finger and thumb. She feels the tips carefully. Maybe she had it cut yesterday and is teaching her fingertips, unused to the sudden, blunt ending, their new reality.

Smoothing my thumb across my fingertips I remember the length of my first ponytail, Morgan's first foetal kicks. She was eager to break free right from the start. I recall the angles of Jonathan's collarbone, hipbone, wristbone. Wishbone. I touch my thumb lightly to each fingertip and remember the enamel colander in my mother's kitchen, how my fingers got stuck in the small holes. And how I would wait patiently until she released them for me.

Walking to the front door, stamping off beach sand from my shoes, I can still see this morning's receding tide with its slow, flat waves spread thinly into silver. A mirror reflecting upside down seagulls. Mounds of jellyfish lay scattered and useless like discarded breast implants; they have been left by the *treknetters*, who cannot avoid dragging them in with the rest of their catch.

My mother's latest mammogram X-ray is slid between the cookbooks in her kitchen.

"It's just a lump, nothing to worry about," Ruth had said last week, taking the X-ray plate from me. "I *am* keeping an eye on it, stop fussing."

Gloria crouches in the shadows behind my eyes like a cancerous growth. Purple grandmother. That is my name for her, the colour of shadows. I balance on a tightrope of tension that exists between us and cannot afford the slackness that forgiveness will bring. This feeling has seeped into my pores, over many years, as if I had eaten too much garlic or onions. Or the smells that settle into your hair when you spend too much time in the kitchen. There was no time before hate.

I hold onto our dark secret, it is a feather stuck in seaweed, and I can't loosen its grip.

Words straddle a fence that runs through my brain. There are two boxes filled with words in there, one on each side of the fence. Small eddies blow and lift them out at random; a word from my father's tongue, *flight,* a word from my mother's tongue, *vrek.* Words to catch and mangle my thoughts. Mangle them until they limp past tongue and teeth.

Sea sand scum skuim ruim raam wind wond wound.

Gloria

The pile of possible gifts for Morgan grows. A length of dark grey satin with embroidered doves, two button-cards, starched collars found in the box under the mirror, a pile of knitting patterns, four spools of coloured thread. And a few blocks of colour, wrapped in Elizabeth's lace handkerchief.

When Ruth was four months old, Gloria bought paints and paper, pencils and watercolour blocks. She stroked the cool ferrules holding the stiff hairs; brushed them against her cheek. Days were spent drawing in the garden, circled by mountains, the laager surrounding the town where she lived with Frankie and her child.

Grass blades, fingers, toes, the crocheted pattern of her lilac shawl; graphite images of these found their way onto white paper; through colour loaded on a wet brush, dripping clouds onto damp paper stretched over a wooden board. She drew her left hand as a limp inanimate object floating above the paper. Images found their way through translucent eyelids. Gloria could see even with her eyes closed.

Ruth crawled on an itchy blanket, straight-legged, her dough-white bottom airing a rash. They sat under a gnarled tree, its growth stunted in that semi-desert climate. Its shade smudged shadows onto the sleeping childface as Gloria lost herself in memories of nights with Frankie, dark moon longings and release as if from thunder and lightning. His secret was locked safe in the embrace of a rubber band cross, tucked inside a wooden box, and placed at the back of Frankie's bedside drawer.

Shapes grew on the blank paper on the easel in front of her, where shadows held the forms captive. The textured marks defined what she imagined. She rubbed and rubbed with a wet finger, roughening the paper to get it right. Hollows formed under her baby's eye on the paper, a dark dimpled chin appeared – it could hold a kiss – and the soft pencil strokes became knotted fur at the back of Ruth's head, where a bald patch eventually appeared.

Frankie teased Ruth, "Daddy's girl . . . my little bald sparrow." And he tickled her under her ribcage. His eyes strayed to Gloria's drawings where they lay on the kitchen table at night, lingering on the tenderness of his daughter's limbs. He traced their outline with his fingertip.

"You need to know where the darkness ends and the light begins," Gloria said, watching him, "to translate reality into art." A warning sparked down her spine; right down to the tailbone that still ached from her daughter's birthing. Gloria's perineum had healed as a lump of scar tissue, but bruised bone takes longer to heal, and a dull throb down there was a constant companion.

"Like the paintings of your father, I suppose," he said, glancing at them where they hung grouped above the fireplace.

"Exactly," she replied. "That artist knew what he was doing."

Ruth rested barebottomed and sunwarmed on her mother's hip, while she spoke nonsense-talk to her child, seldom addressing Frankie directly.

"Let's see what Daddy would like for supper, sweetie, what do you think Daddy would like, my darling?"

Eager mothers brought their reluctant children, ordering portraits for posterity, heirlooms to pass down to their grandchildren. Gloria observed and captured, holding them captive with games, cat's cradle and church's steeple. Frankie helped with his wide crocodile smile, which failed to stir a limbic memory of amphibian fear in the children. His camera recorded plump legs falling open, fowl-like drumsticks, bare bottoms splayed over beach balls, or mounting the black and white rocking horse, babyspit a jewelled thread hanging from their mouths.

Frankie winked at the children, *funnyman,* they thought. Their mothers were absent, lost in the talking pictures jerking darkly across screens those hot afternoons. The toddlers were left with Gloria. She made tea, sometimes went to the bathroom, – and Frankie winked and clicked.

"Let me help you," he said, "I'll look after them."

Morgan

I pour sand over the fire and walk to the compost heap to scrape the butternut remains from my plate. The air carries the smell of rain; in the distance dark clouds are speeding across the sky. I walk back to the shed and fetch the fork leaning against the side.

"Okay, cow, move!" I say, walking to the labyrinth. She lifts her head and stares, chewing long blades of grass. I nudge her with the tip of my shoe. "Come on, I don't have all day."

The cow lumbers away with a soulful moo and I push the fork into the ground, balancing my feet on the narrow metal shoulders and rocking backwards to loosen the hard soil.

"This could take a while," I say to myself. I open the tap, then place the hosepipe at the start of the labyrinth. The water runs inside, softening the soil. Walking to the house to fetch myself a beer, I smile as I remember Timo's reaction when he heard me trying to swear. I take after my grandfather, whose only swearword was *piss-off*.

"Oi?" Timo said, "Oi? This is the best you can do after dropping a rock on your toes?"

Then rattled off a few alternatives that would make even Gloria blush.

After my argument with Isabel over Timo's fashion photography I invited my mother to a shoot for *Bella*, an Italian magazine, promoting new design talent from Africa.

"Come and see for yourself, before you make sweeping statements," I told her.

We drove to the Company Gardens in silence. The closer we get to the date of my departure, the less my mother and I have to say to each other. When we arrived Timo was busy unpacking his cameras and checking his lenses, while a make-up person was dusting the cheeks of one of the models with a shimmering powder. They were grouped at the bottom of the steps in front of the National Gallery. The rectangular stone lily pond below formed the backdrop.

My mother said that she would like to sit on the Gallery steps and watch from a distance. I agreed, relieved that I would be away from her disapproving gaze. I walked with Timo to meet the model, a young girl of about sixteen with very pale hair and skin. She was modelling a range of gypsy-style blouses. Not my thing at all. Too frilly and fussy. A large white screen was placed to her left, and in the reflected light she appeared translucent.

A short woman with black cropped hair, almost seal-like, approached. "Fantastic!" she shouted, throwing her arms up in the air. She walked over to Timo and kissed him. A bit too long and hard for my liking, but I am not the jealous type.

"Only nine o'clock and so hot already!" she said, her English syrup-coated with an Italian accent. She took off her T-shirt. Underneath it she was wearing what looked like a sports bra to me, she arched back, sliding the palms of her hands down the back of her thighs.

"Heaven! Bliss!" she said, inhaling deeply as she uncurled her body again. I wondered what my mother made of all of this.

After an eternity of fussing with hair and make-up and lights and light meters they were finally ready. By now Timo was dripping with sweat. He pulled his T-shirt over his head and smiled at the model, posed and ready.

"Beautiful," he said, and clicked.

I walk outside and lean the empty beer bottle against the wall of the fireplace, then close the tap. My hair is longer than I have ever worn it, and I try to catch every strand in the hair band before leaning my weight onto the fork. This time the tines sink in deep around the base of the largest weedy shrub. The soil releases the roots of the plant with a satisfying crunch.

Gloria

Gloria walked to the low crumbling wall that formed the back boundary of their property. The wall was a crooked line of collapsed stone; more sand than stone, and stiff weeds caught on her stockings. She cursed.

Rose petal scabs lay on the ground next to her.

With clenched knuckles she rubbed her eyes roughly and the blue smear of sky distorted through the wetness. Tears flowed backwards down her throat, she swallowed. As she turned to look at her house, she fingered the fragment of mirror in her skirt pocket. Cataract windows, reflecting the clouds, stared blindly back at her.

Frankie's seed was drying on her thighs.

His secret was obscured inside the house, where she had found him with the pile of photographs, the rubber band that held them lying limp on the bedside table. The children were posed to tempt and tease, and his arousal was clearly visible. Her own desire shivered to the surface of her skin, through raised hair follicles, coursing hotly through arteries. Taking a crêpe bandage from the drawer, Frankie wound it around her eyes, "Shh . . . " he said, "You don't have to look."

Together they tumbled, photographs sticking like stamps to their damp nakedness, her soft belly rippling under his touch, and yes, there was pain after all. She slapped him hard, hand on bristly cheek.

"This is a trap!" she cried out, panic-struck.

"You are an accomplice now," he hissed, "Shut up!"

She tore the bandage from her eyes and pleaded, her voice

low, "Ruth," she whispered, "Have you ever?"

"Never," he said, "You have my word. In any case, I don't hurt them . . . what do they know?"

Gloria stood shivering in front of Frankie; he stroked her arm, spoke softly, "It's harmless, the lens of the camera doesn't hurt, the only caress is from a lens. I don't touch the children. I never have."

She suddenly saw what it was that he had always hidden from her, and her life disintegrated into pieces of a puzzle that fell randomly, the image, the pattern destroyed – and nothing fitted any longer.

Gloria placed a petal, rose-bitter, in her mouth, biting a hole through its centre for her tongue. Taking the tiny mirror from her pocket – keeper of mother's eyes and mother's mouth – she saw the obscene organ poking through.

"Witch-bitch-fleshwound-stitch-earth-stone-death-bone," she whispered, and the torn petal fell to the ground.

She stared back at the house and thought of Ruth asleep in her crib, dreaming of feathers falling. The sky paled from cerulean to the pearlescent hue of a stretched balloon. Fat clouds drifted by. Gloria lay down under the tree and sleep snatched a memory that struggled to surface through the blue. She dreamt of Frankie standing on the balcony outside their bedroom window staring at her as she slept. His mouth was sewn closed with thick black thread. His oily stare coated her skin and she saw his smooth, hairless hands with red fingernails, talon-claws, pulling Ruth's smocked dress down, smoothing it over her dimpled knees.

She saw his tears dripping like acid onto his camera as he placed it in the dark brown case.

"Ma-ma!" she heard Ruth calling, and started awake. Cradling her daughter, her husband was walking towards her, ducking under the nameless tree. Ruth leaned away from Frankie, towards Gloria, almost falling from her father's arms.

Ruth

She pulls the last box from the sitting room into the kitchen, and cuts through the packing tape with a sharp knife. The bread tins are at the top, wedged between pots and pans. Gloria's cake tins are pushed down the side of the box. They are rusted and useless, but Ruth has kept them anyway, even had to sneak them past Isabel's eyes. She takes them out and places them next to the scales on the table.

Her mother baked whenever she felt her anger rise. It never calmed her down, though, and only increased the intensity and heat that built up inside her until it boiled over.

As she looks at the two pans, the familiar emotion that had risen whenever she watched her mother bake, wells in her now. It is as if she is about to remember a dream. But Ruth never remembers her dreams. She awakens to the feelings they leave behind. Regret and sadness. Attempting to remember dis-members; the details are pushed underground, and remain buried.

How do I know that what I remember is the truth, she muses as she pushes the pans into the rubbish bag. Shards from the vinyl record slice through the plastic and she fetches another, stronger bag. She can smell Gloria's burnt baking on her fingers, under the brown rust dust of the pan.

Without closing her eyes, she can see her mother, standing at her kitchen table late in the afternoon, baking cakes.

Sweat was pooled in the gully between Gloria's breasts. Eleven cakes were already standing on the table, and she bent down to take the last one out. As the heat of the oven hit her, she swore.

"Twelve cakes!" Ruth squealed, counting, "Are we having a party?"

But her mother didn't look at her, nor did she answer. Pulling a mixing bowl closer, she opened a packet of icing sugar and poured it in. Three aloe leaves lay next to the bowl on the table. Ruth watched in silence as her mother scraped away the blue-green surface of the leaves with a sharp knife, then, with a fork, mashed the skinned leaves into a stringy pulp.

"Let him drink from the bitter cup," she told Ruth, "Useless man, dull man, brought filth into my house, corrupt. I'll show him, teach him a lesson!"

She mixed the bitter pulp with the icing sugar, and added spoons of salt with the dark cocoa powder, ruining it.

"Why should he feel no pain?" she asked.

She prepared one sweet cake; to offer Frankie a chance, a choice, and fetched a packet of glazed cherries from the fridge.

"You can put them on," she told Ruth, passing the packet to her, "One on each cake."

Frankie entered and reddened at the sight of twelve red cherry nipples glistening back at him.

"Yes!" Gloria shouted, "This is what I have been doing, baked the demons out of me, isn't that how you would put it?"

Ruth watched as her father emptied out his pockets, avoiding her mother's eyes.

"Damn you!" Gloria erupted, slamming the knife blade into the surface of the table. "Cut a slice, see if you can find the good one, see if you can manage to do something right today," she said, picking up the glass next to her.

Frankie walked past her and bumped the glass from her hand.

"You drunk, useless bitch," he said, softly, and lifted Ruth away from the shards.

They left Gloria standing next to the table, roaring into the night outside. Ruth heard the sound of the breaking plates and started to cry. Frankie walked up and down the passage, rocking her in his arms, "Shh-shh," he said, "It's just a dream, go back to sleep."

*

Ruth woke up inside a dream one morning a week after David had left her. *I am in love,* she thought, smiling into her pillow. She could feel the pressure of a warm hand on her back, guiding her through a dance. Her legs were tangled with the twisted sheets.

The sound of tango music drained away and was replaced by that of the neighbour's son's percussion practise.

Isabel

I enter the kitchen and switch on the kettle. Then lean against the counter and watch its small orange light glow in the dimness. I feel dizzy after my walk – this day feels far too complicated.

A row of ants forms a black line against the stone wall behind the kettle. They exit from, and return to, a gap above the plugpoint. My mother cursed these black lines in her kitchen. "Go crawl somewhere else," she said, and rubbed lemon juice over all the surfaces to chase them away.

"Ants don't crawl," I told her, "They move too fast."

I needed a word that would describe their frantic running on unseen legs, forming a fluid line of ant bodies on the wall; two lines going in opposite directions, briefly sniffing and bumping heads, like friendly dogs on the beach. Do ants ever sleep, I wondered. I imagined tiny eyelashes surrounding tiny eyes. Do they live long enough to need to?

Still searching for the right word, I found one for the sound of birdwing against a closed window, a frantic, flapping word. *Fludder.* It was a perfect sound-marriage between words from both my tongues: *Vladder* and shudder. Trapped birds fluddered against the kitchen window all the time.

Watching their escape attempts, a memory seemed to slip, like a pressed flower petal falling from the pages of my Bible. I followed its trajectory until it landed on the red earth underneath the Brazilian pepper tree in my grandfather's garden. Once more I saw the child tugging at a drawer; this time it opened and a wooden box fell out. The petal became a bloodstained handkerchief and floated onto a waxy green carpet of flowers.

Bee humming filled my ears.

I sat on the edge of my mother's kitchen table, too big, now, to sit cross-legged on top. I just sat, and looked at the rows of ants running blindly on the wall.

Tonguefused.

*

Dog's meowing gets me moving, and I walk to Morgan's closed room. The cat is waiting at the door and arches his back in a purry greeting.

"Hello, Dog," I say, picking him up, "You don't mind your silly name, hey, boy . . . there you go . . . into your basket . . . I won't be long."

I carry the basket with me to the kitchen and put it on the table, then walk to the sink to wash the beach smells from my hands.

Jonathan jogs every morning from our house, past Wooley's pool and the harbour, up Clairvaux Road, into Boyes Drive. Up Ponder Steps where the black crow sits and waits, past the small waterfall, an early seasonal trickle after last week's rain. Just past the waterfall he usually leaves the road and jogs right up the mountain, into Echo Valley. I don't follow him there because I am a walker. A one-foot-in-front-of-the-other-woman who could walk right around the world if only I had the time.

Jonathan pants into the kitchen just as I pour water into the coffee plunger.

"I am too old for this!"

He has been saying this for the last five years.

"Think how much older you'd feel if you didn't do this."

142

Familiar phrases, smoothed-pebble talk.

He smiles.

"I suppose so. But we don't know that for sure."

He reaches for a glass and pours water into it, drains it in one long gulp.

"A scientific experiment would require the same person to jog and not to jog for – say – twenty years simultaneously. Of course, that can't be done. Science can't determine the benefits, if any, of the road not taken. Pour me some?"

He indicates the coffee and sits down at the table. Takes a sip and reaches for more milk.

"Sorry," I say.

I never make his coffee milky enough.

"How was your walk?"

"Good. It was a good walk. I brought you this."

I take the swollen Norfolk Pine seed from my pocket and place it on his outstretched hand. I put the shell on the table, saying, "It looks a bit like barbed clitoris, don't you think?"

He blushes at this and peers at the seed more closely.

"Really, Isabel, where do you get your ideas from?"

"Same place as you, I suppose."

He closes his fingers around the seed and puts it in his pocket.

"I wish I'd never had this table stripped and cleaned," I say, sitting down next to Jonathan. I wrap my cold hands around the mug. "I never thought he'd die so suddenly, so soon."

David had given me the table when he moved out of my mother's house.

"It's the only thing I want from her," he told me, "I made it, after all."

Cleaning the table had removed all the memories and marks worked into a patina of age and dirt. The bloodstain is no longer visible. I had thought we would have time together to create new memories, that we could put a new layer of wax down and polish it, together, to a soft sheen. And that we would finally talk, because my father and I both needed our hands to be busy for our thoughts to stir. Traces of the scribbles in the corner, where he once explained the basic principles of electricity to me, are still there.

"Well, you had no way of knowing," Jonathan says, "You'll just have to make new memories."

He pulls Morgan's party list closer. "Are you going to be okay tonight?"

I bounce the question back, feeling my eyebrows rise in defence. "Are you?"

He shrugs, "It's hard," he says, scanning the list.

"I never told you about that fashion shoot I went to, last week, in the Gardens – "

"Oh yes, I meant to ask you, did Morgan manage to convince you?"

"No, it proved my point, but of course she would disagree."

"I think the two of you are at each other's throats to make parting easier, when it comes."

"We're not exactly at each other's throats, you know. I just happen to be right in this case. Looking at the shoot from the back gave me a special viewpoint that day. I sat on the steps of the gallery and watched from there. I tell you, I was just amazed at the whole set-up, the lies and subterfuge – "

"Aren't you exaggerating just a little bit, Isabel?"

"I think if you'd been there you'd agree with me . . . the model was so thin that not even the smallest blouse they had would fit her. So they just pinned it at the back, with safety pins, it was pathetic to watch . . . and of course she had no boobs, I mean, honestly! Gypsy clothing needs some healthy flesh, don't you agree?"

"Of course I do," he smiled and popped some bread in the toaster.

"So they had to slip two gel-filled bags into her bra-cups to

144

give her some cleavage. I actually felt like crying, you know, looking at that bony girl with her winged shoulder blades, prodded and pinned to fit some screwed-up ideal of beauty."

"Did you tell Morgan how you felt? How you saw it?"

"There was never a right moment, and anyway, she's so in love with Timo, I doubt she noticed anything other than him. Shirtless and dripping with sweat as he was."

The toast popped, and I fetched plates from the drying rack next to the sink. Jonathan opened the fridge door and put butter and cheese on the table. He picked up my list.

"Do you really think that buying every food item she has ever liked might make her stay?" he teases, then reads it out loud. "Chocolate cake, raspberry coldrink, pineapple pizza, honey and mustard pretzels, roti bread, hummus and tahini, falafel balls, stuffed green olives. Salad stuff, cheese straws from the farm stall – "

I take the list from him. "The one guarantee we have is very bad indigestion. I'd better rethink this."

Our only child is leaving the country in two weeks, maybe forever. From then on it will be different. We can't follow her, can't already start planning our first visit, although every cell in my body is already straining to do just that. Morgan will leave and we will remain. Turned into ghost crabs scuttling about at low tide, slithering back to the water. All the unspoken thoughts we could hide in our daughter will be exposed.

Jonathan pours more coffee into his mug and says, "I have fewer regrets than you do. Morgan and you are too close; you can't see each other properly – like when you make one owl-eye by touching noses with a friend? Have you ever done that?"

"I'm just glad that we're having her party tonight. I need to say goodbye now so that I can let her go when she actually goes, know what I mean?"

"Like having a funeral before the death? To get it over with?"

"Not quite, but yes, I suppose so."

145

We finish our breakfast in silence. Jonathan walks to the shower and I look at Morgan's party list. At the top of the page her name is scrolled in a gold and purple flourish. I have been preparing for tonight ever since my daughter announced her decision to go to Scotland. It feels as if my father had gone before Morgan, as if David will be waiting for Morgan at Edinburgh airport when she arrives. They were always close. Sometimes love and affection need to skip a generation to find expression.

Between my father and me there was always a tension created by the unsaid, rather than by the said.

Morgan has cut the last strand of umbilical cord and is leaving it to me to expel the afterbirth. No more hiding, no more hanging on.

I could have asked Ruth to prepare all the food, but I need to do this myself. I pour a second cup of coffee. Make a list. Another one. When in doubt, make a list. Ruth's rule, inherited from Frankie, who loved making lists for everything.

My rule is, when in doubt, wash. Like Jennie the cat in Paul Gallico's book. Did I ever give my old copy to Morgan, I wonder. Jonathan often finds the bath running at odd hours during the day because that is my automatic response to stress: have a bath. I decide to do just that, and, scooping up the pages, pen and coffee, I walk to the bathroom.

An hour later Jonathan has left for work. He put the seed I gave him in his jacket pocket, close to the photograph, and the poem. He kissed me and walked out the door. He is giving a lecture today about seed dispersal patterns along the Western Cape shoreline and I know that he will take the seed out and put it on top of his notes, touching it absentmindedly throughout. He will think of me.

Gloria

With Ruth balanced on her hip, Gloria walked back to the house and through the kitchen door. Honey-light spilled over copper pots hanging, hooked. Frankie entered with a gift, and taking Ruth from Gloria, handed her an oblong package.

"What is this? It's so heavy."

She poured a large whisky and gulped it down to quench her sleepwoken thirst.

"Come on," he said, gesturing with his head, "Open it."

He took the glass from Gloria, who wondered if it was another stolen gift, shoplifted from Wolhuter & Sons, carefully noted in the red book inside his coat pocket where he recorded all the small items taken over the past months.

Frankie was a careful accountant, always making lists, recording every transgression. His stolen gifts piled up in boxes stuffed into cupboards. Button-cards and linen collars lay starched and stiff in white boxes, smelling of mothballs. Balls of wool, soft and red, rested on top.

The oblong box lay in her hands, heavy with destiny.

"Open it!" he urged, impatient.

"I'll keep it, it's so pretty," Gloria said as she fingered the fine paper. She revealed a lidded box, made from pale wood. The lid slid out like that of her first-grade pencil box. She remembered an apple in her school suitcase, forgotten, pulpsmear against her books, and opened the lid to reveal a metal U-shape.

"Oh . . . a magnet!" She looked up at Frankie, questioningly.

"No, no," he approached, reproached, putting Ruth down at their feet. The toddler rocked backwards and forwards, straining for balance.

"See, there is more," he said, revealing a smaller box deep inside, filled with iron filings. He poured these onto a stiff sheet of white paper, and moved the magnet underneath to tease out jumpy clumps of darkness, assembling and disassembling at random, like a tea-leaf reading.

"Could this predict our future?" she asked him, teasing.

Later it became a game for the children. Some found it frightening, the jumpy black shapes too spider-like, moved along by Gloria's unseen hand under the paper.

By now, alcohol was her constant companion, liquid medication. She imagined her father judging her from somewhere beyond, while she floated in a world of colour and pretended a happy life. She propped her easel among the roots of the nameless tree, and the pictures she drew were increasingly dark. The children fidgeted and squirmed, sensing her withdrawal. The mothers, apprehensive, refused to pay for the strange portraits.

The children seemed to drown on the paper in smears of charcoal.

"Where is she? Where is Anna?" a mother asked. "This doesn't look like Deon!" said another. Gloria laughed her amber breath into their narrowed eyes, pointing at the dim shadows on the page and said, "Don't you know where your children are?" she screamed into their deaf ears, "Why don't you know where your children are?"

Ruth

Scanning through the list of ingredients she needs to bake two loaves of Farmhouse Bread, she realises that she would have to go to the corner café to buy yeast. Cooking with yeast has always been pleasurable to her; kneading the aromatic dough is relaxing. And it still gives her a strange thrill to peep under the wet cloth at the expanding cream-coloured shape.

With her purse in her coat pocket she locks the door behind her and walks the half-block to the shop. She passes a woman with an alcohol-ravished face who reminds her of Gloria. She is a well-known *bergie*, as the homeless are called in Cape Town, and the only neighbour she has spoken to since her move. "When I come back I'll give you something," she says. "No money?" the woman asks, holding out her hands. Ruth shakes her head.

Soon after that bitter-baking day, her father had come home holding a pale blue letter in his hand. Again, wife and daughter were in the kitchen, waiting.

Or is she just imagining this Ruth wonders, entering the shop. Because she herself was always in the kitchen with Isabel, waiting? But she sees her mother's hands inside the cream-coloured mixing bowl, stuck inside the dough. She sees her jutting her chin forward in an attempt to blow a fly off her nose; lifting her shoulders into a shrug to shake it off.

Gloria's eyes met those of Frankie, who had just entered the room. They flashed an accusation.

"Can't you see I'm stuck?" she said.

She blew at the air with a jutting bottom lip. Ruth pushed out her own bottom lip, trying to see if it was the same strange colour as her mother's. Her father walked to the table and put down a card filled with mother-of-pearl-buttons.

When no one was looking, Gloria told Ruth, Frankie slid small items into his pockets at Wolhuter's. He worked too hard and was paid too little. That was his excuse, her mother told her.

Her father brought these stolen items home to his waiting wife to placate her, to soften her anger. The previous week he had brought knitting patterns for a blue cape, a yellow romper, a red coat trimmed with angora. Also buttons and balls of red wool. And crochet needles.

But he entered the kitchen too late, the small gift of buttons would not work their magic that day. The card looked diminished and ridiculous, lying next to the mixing bowl with white flour dusted on top. Gloria's mood was already ruined by the time he arrived home. By the stickiness of the dough, the fly, the heat inside her that she always complained about.

Dishes remained unwashed in the sink behind her, as she squinted at the green kitchen scales in front of her, as if trying to measure out her day.

Ruth looked up at her mother and noticed that her cheeks seemed higher in her face than usual, her eyes almost shut. Frankie shoved the pale blue envelope in front of Gloria's face. He loosened the knot of his tie. Her mother started humming through her nose, a single note that skidded drunkenly into the air. "Oh!" she laughed, bumping into a chair, "I am drunk as a skunk musty-musty paint in the trunk – "

He put the letter down in front of her. "Can't you speak like a normal person?" he asked.

"Maybe. I. will. *never*. speak. again," she said, cocking her head from side to side.

"Let's bake cookies, Mommy!" Ruth grabbed her mother's hand, her face serious and frowning. Gloria turned to Frankie and cleared her throat. Attempted a smile. Her eyes were mere slits by then, like the homeless woman's leaning against the wall of the shop. "My God, why can't this child of ours ever smile?" she asked.

"Mommy . . . !" Ruth tugged at her mother's skirt. Gloria got up and leaned with her hands on the table. She picked up the letter.

"No sweetie, just play and leave Mommy alone."

Ruth watched her mother's tears slide into the glass and fished an ice-cube out with her fingers; almost choked, and coughed and spluttered, then let the warmth of her mouth melt it.

Gloria read the letter out loud. "Dear Mr Moss, this time we cannot let you off with a warning, blah blah . . . has come to our attention – " She shook her head at her husband. "You stupid, stupid man," she said, her eyes scanning the rest of the letter, before she let it fall to the floor.

Frankie whooped Ruth upwards to the ceiling, suddenly brave, suddenly quite the man. "Time for a fresh start!" he said, "Time to move on, time to leave this godforsaken place!"

Ruth's hand covered her mouth, the "Oh!" escaping unheard. Her mother looked at Frankie, and said, "The stone wall and the nameless tree, the roses – everything – are you asking me to leave it all behind? Were you caught red-handed this time?"

Her father didn't answer, just slipped the loosened tie over his head, and his jacket from his shoulders.

"Let's try our luck in Cape Town!" said the big man, grinning nervously, nodding when Gloria asked, "My father's house by the sea?"

After licking the mixing spoon, Ruth rolled the sweetness around her mouth with her tongue. She pressed pale dough into a square tin, humming tunelessly under her breath to block out her mother's words.

"Only last week I told the child that we must try and stay above it all, that you are the cross I have to bear . . . Ruthie, what did Mommy tell you!"

Ruth watched as her mother crumbled her way through each day, morning to noon, noon to night. Messing it up, turning it into a sticky page from a child's homework book.

Frankie walked up to Gloria, his hand knocking against the bottle in front of her as he tried to pull her from her chair. Holding her by the shoulder, and with his lips almost touching her ear, he said, "Sugar and drink, is this what you live on?"

Ruth looked at her father and wondered why his voice became softer and softer whenever her mother's became louder and louder.

"Shame on you," he said, removing his hand. Gloria wobbled back onto the seat of the chair. "And the child doing all the cooking and the baking in this house."

"And all the eating," Gloria laughed, prodding the soft flesh of her daughter's waist. For Ruth would often sneak food from her mother's untouched plate. And so, as her thighs plumped out, the child came to gestate the mother, eating for both of them.

"I feel dizzy, Mom," Ruth said when Frankie left the kitchen. She rested her head against her mother's knee. "And my head hurts."

Gloria touched Ruth's head with her hand, then pushed her towards the oven.

"If you don't watch the biscuits dear, they'll burn."

Isabel

I have a new, improved list in my left jacket pocket. Keys and cellphone in the right pocket. I scan the list and see that it looks competent and business-like. Gone is the fancy scrolling around Morgan's name. The to-do and to-buy lists have merged into one sensible sequence.

- Take Dog to the cattery.
- Drive to Chart Farm to pick roses. (Yellow). Do I have enough vases?
- Go to Ruth (have tea?). Remind her to fetch Gloria tonight. Borrow some vases. Fetch wine.
- Phone Morgan to remind her about extra linen. Ask about Timo. (Whether he is coming)
- Pick 'n Pay.
- Try and find more fairy lights.
- Home.
- Drive to McGregor.

As I open the front door to walk to my car I hear desperate meowing. I forgot all about Dog, sitting in the cat basket on the table. I fetch the basket and place him next to me, on the passenger seat.

I have no real sense of direction, but whenever I drive along the road that leads to Cape Point I see myself from above, as if I am flying above the tar. My station wagon becomes a crawling insect – grey on grey. I see vast oceans on both sides of the finger of land curving southward. Driving along this road gives me a sense of knowing exactly where I am on the contours of

153

the African continent. The feeling is immediate and exhilarating. Will Morgan be able to match the DNA of her soulmap to the foreign geography of Scotland?

I fly above the tar road that cuts through the heartscape of fynbos and sandstone and arum lily. Guinea fowl and suikerbos.

Morgan claims that this landscape holds no meaning for her.

"It's just a place, Mom, stop making such a fuss."

These are words I hear often.

"My soul connection is to stone. And Scotland has that in abundance."

Some throwback gene from David's side of the family is calling my daughter back to Scotland. It is from David that Morgan has inherited the gene that gives a thumb the ability to flex backwards in an arch, and he in turn inherited this from his mother. Maybe that is the gene that links Morgan to the soul of Scotland.

The late summer fires, fanned by hot bergwinds, have left huge scars on the mountainside, with powder-grey ash hovering like a ghostly presence. Soft greens are pushing through in the relentless cycle of life and death. Here and there, fire lilies are already flaming through the ash.

A line of washing streams past in my peripheral vision. White cloth nappies hang next to brightly coloured Babygros, the small legs and arms dancing in the wind. The space between the steering wheel and my body warms to a memory of Morgan, fed and burped, a compact six-month old body resting on my belly. There were endless loads of washing, and Jonathan helped with the folding of sheets.

No more nappies, but the sheets remain.

A dead snake lies in the road, flattened and stuck to the tar by broad tyre tracks. I downshift to second gear, slowing down in order to drive around it.

I am the only driver on this stretch of road. I no longer trust my instincts, and wonder whether I would have come this way if I had read about a car hijacking or an ambush on this road yesterday. I am having a conversation with my mother. We are in a dream kitchen, with black marble countertops and a stainless steel fridge.

"Cheer up!" she says as I tell her about the snake. "Look on the bright side!" An image flashes before my eyes; my mother skating soundlessly over the floor of her kitchen, barely cutting the surface. She is wearing the paper-doll clothes I imagined for her when I was little, with a white apron fastened over the skirt of her dress. Battle-dress, ready for action. I catch a glimpse of my own face, next to that of my father. We are trapped reflections in the polished surface of her kitchen floor.

I breathe out, and adjust my seatbelt.

"Let's talk about your grandfather," I hear my mother say. I see that she is holding a paper-thin tomato carver in her hand. Bits of red wet the steel. I slow down again, this time for a row of nervous guinea fowl that twitter across the road.

"Come on," my mother invites, "sit down."

The silence in the car knits into conversation. Becomes speech with meaning. A tight weave that allows little light through as we talk about grandfathers. They are mostly skulls now. Buried deep in the earth, with their long white bones round-ended and smooth. Thy have returned to dust, fed back into the soil.

"Well," I say, "you know how you often left me with Gloria and Frankie when I was little?"

I stop talking as the sound of Dog's low nervous growl fills the car. Winding down the window, I let in some air and inhale deeply.

"I used to love leaning my cheek against his coat pocket, it was rough and smelled of XXX Mints. I sometimes slid my hand inside his pocket and stole some. I am sure he must've known what I was up to, but he let me do it anyway."

The hairs on the back of my neck rise in memory of his hot, whispered words explaining Gloria's drunkenness and verbal abuse. "You'll have to excuse her," he said as he stroked my cheek with a rough-edged thumb, breathing the words into my ear, "Never mind her, she is ill, she doesn't know what she is saying." I rub the memory of his touch away, away from the round edge of my jawbone, just below my ear.

I would hide the stolen mints in my wooden playhouse outside my mother's kitchen. Once I had outgrown the table top, I sat on the concrete floor outside this little house, passing time. Or cracking open walnuts, smashing them with a black stone. They were always rotten, filled with worm eggs threaded together in gritty clumps.

"Did you love your grandfather?"

"What?" I turn my head sharply towards the crouching cat, accusing it of speech. "What did you say?"

The sharp knife slices into the skin of a ripe tomato. "Did you love your grandfather?" she asks again.

As a child, I loved the plump rise of her breasts, their cleft visible above the top button of the V-necked blouses she wore. She smelled of roses. I inhaled her when she lifted me from the table. My mother's clothes appeared in my mind as generic paper-doll clothes, with blank rectangles on the shoulders to attach the clothes. Neat dresses with pinched waists. Plain coloured blouses, never patterned, except for the one red polka dot shirt she wore with a wide-belted blue skirt. She always wore an apron over her normal day-clothes, white and spotless.

"He gave me peppermints whenever I wanted some. I smelled like a secret smoker at age eight. Remember his fifty-second birthday? In 1952 it was, I remember because he aged along with the century."

We were having lunch at my grandparents' house, to celebrate his birthday, sitting under the Brazilian Pepper tree in their back garden. My mother said the word "Verwoerd," often, which at the time sounded to me like the Afrikaans word *woedend*. I knew that it meant being very very angry. I imagined Brolloks, the angry cannibal I found on the pages of a book inside my grandfather's bookcase.

"The Langenhoven story of *Brolloks en Bittergal* was my favourite," I tell my mother now, glancing in Dog's direction, co-opting him as a silent listener.

The car becomes a confessional.

"Remember how he kept his books in that special bookcase, the one with lead glass doors? To me they looked like the windows of a castle. The story of *Brolloks en Bittergal* was set in the *grasveld* Karoo landscape, lots of flat land surrounded by mountains."

Wiping the tomato pulp from the blade of the knife between forefinger and thumb, my mother waits for me to continue.

"In one of the mountains was a cave where Brolloks lived. He was described as a *mensvreter en towernaar*."

I remember the chills I felt reading that word – *vreter* – the word conjured up an image of blood dripping from teeth, tearing at flesh. My mother wipes her hands on her apron as I continue.

"Brolloks was a cannibal and a sorcerer. He held a young girl captive in his cave, after stealing her from her parents one night. In Langenhoven's words, she was *so mooi soos die sterretjies, so mooi soos die watertjies . . . jy kon haar byna 'n engeltjie noem . . . haar hartjie was sag en teer en vol liefde vir die blommetjies en die diertjies.*"

I memorised those descriptions, wanting to be that fragile girl who was as pretty as little stars, and little streams of water, and little angels, her little heart filled with love for the little flowers and little animals. I stop talking to give my mother time to respond, but she remains silent.

"I went inside to find something more interesting to do than listen to the grown-ups' arguments, I was thirsty after drawing in the dust underneath the tree."

Tightening my grip on the steering wheel, I feel the gritty texture of the waxy green seeds that lay under the tree, providing colour for my drawing.

I close the car window, shutting out the cold air, shutting out my mother. The retreating shape of a tall eight-year-old child replaces her image. I watch as the child enters a kitchen, and stretches on tiptoe to reach the tap, cupping cold water straight into her mouth. I see her walk down a passage, wiping her mouth and sitting down next to a glass-fronted bookcase. She reads the story of *Brolloks en Bittergal*, then opens the fattest encyclopaedia in the bookcase. I see the child's finger underlining the longest word on each page. After a while she gives a bored sigh and gets up, then walks to her grandparents' bedroom.

She sits down on their high bed, tilting her ears to the excited voices still arguing outside, just managing with the tip of her toes to touch the heart of a deep red rose, woven into the pattern of the carpet.

The thick green curtains were drawn against the summer sun. My grandparents' bedroom smelled of cigarettes, peppermint and dust. Sitting on their bed, I imagined a whiff of mincemeat-on-toast, grandfather's cooking. I picked up the tumbler on Frankie's bedside cabinet, gave it a sniff, and pulled a face as I remembered his false teeth.

My heart beating wildly, I opened the top drawer. This, I remember, was the first time I had knowingly done anything wrong, unlike other times when Ruth informed me after the fact, that I had been a bad girl.

Inside the drawer was a pile of ironed handkerchiefs. The top one was a faded blue, with light brown stains on it – maybe blood. Next to the handkerchiefs was a white box filled with mother-of-pearl buttons. My fingers pushed in among their brittle coolness, as I listened all the while for a change in the voices outside.

I pushed my hand deeper into the drawer, and it stopped short against a wooden partition. Pulling the entire drawer out, I discovered the separate compartment that Frankie had made to keep his secret safe. I lifted the lid from the wooden box that fitted snugly into the back of the drawer, and stared at the contents. My eyes knew what they were seeing, but my brain refused to understand. In the top photograph I saw a baby and a woman, older than my mother was at the time, posed naked against velvet cushions. In another photograph I recognised myself as the baby, sitting on my grandmother's lap. My head leaned back between two large breasts, pillowing my ears. Dark nipples rested on Gloria's forearms as she held me. My plump baby legs were held open, revealing the soft walnut of my girlhood. That dark, secret place Ruth had told me never to touch.

I stopped breathing and felt my throat thicken. I lay the photo on the bed and took care to put everything back exactly as I had found it, smoothed the crumpled bed covering, and walked out of the dim bedroom. Not knowing what else to do, I tore the photograph into small pieces, and ate it.

The wine-mellowed grown-ups were still sitting under the humming tree. I almost managed to convince myself that I had just woken from a bad dream, after falling asleep under the tree, but the scratchiness in my throat told me otherwise.

The grandfathers have returned to dust, but dust has a way of getting into one's eyes and streaking them with tears.

Gloria

G loria uses the length of embroidered grey satin to wrap all the items on her bed. She has given up trying to decide what to take for Morgan tonight, and what to leave behind.

She always gave Frankie drawings as birthday gifts, and was busy working on one for his fifty-second birthday party when Ruth and David arrived, asking her and Frankie to look after Isabel for the evening.

As soon as they had left, Frankie took Isabel's hand and walked her down the passage towards the kitchen. Gloria heard him say, as they passed the table where she sat, "Your grandmother is in a state of disrepair." He offered an apologetic smile, eyes wide and eyebrows arched, then bent down and whispered something into Isabel's ear.

Gloria started taunting him, dancing drunkenly around him and prodding him in his back with her pencil. Her eyes were red and weepy. Inside her was the same fire that made her bake twelve cakes on a long-ago day, ruining them with bitter icing, and she remembered a knife blade stuck in the unexpectedly soft and yielding surface of the table. Pulling it free, she thrust it towards her husband's face, but restrained herself as the slash flashed in her mind's eye – she could see the peeling away of skin to the flesh underneath, vermilion mixed with china white.

Frankie shrugged her prodding pencil away, and glanced at Isabel, with the corners of his mouth turned down. As if to say, "I told you so . . . this has nothing to do with us." He took Isabel's hand and led her to the kitchen where she would help him make savoury mincemeat to eat with toast.

After a while, Gloria followed them, shouting, "You couldn't even fuck your grandchild if you tried, you limp bastard!" Her words spun him around, but he was busy chopping onions when she entered and she couldn't tell if those were real tears.

"Never mind her," again bending low and speaking into Isabel's ear, "She doesn't know what she is saying."

He walked to the kitchen door and closed it, shutting Gloria out.

She walked back to her drawing, wiping tears away from her cheeks. Imagined the bitter taste of aloe juice sliding into her mouth. She spat, and words slid out, "Goddammit-shit-runt-cunt-whore-bore!"

*

Gloria pulls the small overnight bag from under her bed, and walks to her tall chest-of-drawers. She takes out a pile of underpants, a vest, a roll of pantyhose and two sets of pyjamas. They will all be staying at the farm for three nights, and Ruth warned her to pack enough clothes. From the cupboard she fetches two jerseys, a dressing gown, three blouses, a skirt and a blue dress she doesn't recognise. She sniffs it before placing it on the bed.

"Such a fuss," she mutters, "It's time to go, I think. I am ready."

She remains standing next to the closed suitcase. Her arms hang limply from her shoulders. She closes her eyes and sways gently, like a leaf that is about to fall.

Isabel

I am part of the traffic organism; this large beast with its belly slung low in a steady crawl forward. My arms pushed straight against the steering wheel, I think of the thousands of hands resting limply on steering wheels, all over the city; feet on pedals: clutch, petrol, brake, clutch. The easiest thing on earth would be to accelerate and ram into the car in front. I keep my distance – only a fool breaks the two-second rule.

Thoughts float in the warm car like decapitated daisies in a bowl of water. Morgan's way of displaying flowers. No sentimental swaying on stalks for her. Off with their heads instead!

In a dream last night, I tried to buy flowers in a shop that doesn't sell flowers. A woman in a white apron offered to pick some in her garden. I watched as she cut the thick green stems at ground level, shaking off the dark earth as she handed them to me. The aproned woman didn't seem to notice that the flower heads were filigreed lace after the worms and moths had feasted on them. She handed them to me like a precious gift and I accepted the dead flowers, stroking the patches of shredded colour. The stalks were throbbing with life. The palms of my hands grew warm and I woke up with clenched fists.

Near the turn-off into the dirt road that will take me to the cattery, I slow down, passing tall bluegum trees. They are naturalised aliens in this African landscape. A sign is fixed to one peeling trunk, *Fynbos Cattery and Kennels*. I stop and reverse the car, then turn into the bumpy dirt road to which Dog objects with a low growling moan. A feeling of regret flashes through me when I realise I won't see the cat again after today.

Morgan had brought Dog home after the time she spent at the farm with David, and I have looked after him often since then. I park the car next to the stables and get out. As I lift the cat basket out Mrs Robinson trots down the steps to take it from me. There has always been a strange animosity between us and I am pleased that I will no longer have to try to unravel this. Before I can speak, she says, "Just give me the basket. It's all arranged. Morgan's friend will pay me when he collects the cat. Off you go, no need to come in." She shoos me away like a yard chicken and I hand her the basket.

"Well, I'm off then, goodbye," I offer to her retreating back. Mrs Robinson is already halfway up the steps.

I turn the car around and bump down to the tar. To the freedom of grey ribbon stretching out in front of me.

I have a recurring daymare when driving in my car. I see myself approaching a four-way intersection, but cannot find the brake pedal. My right foot refuses to release the accelerator. I speed through the stop sign, and through another, and another.

How many times could I do this and remain unharmed, I wonder, if I choose to turn daymare into reality.

Sometimes, while driving, another daymare enters my mind. One moment I'll be driving along – home, shop, library, home – then suddenly find myself face to face with a burglar in my kitchen. I invite him to sit down and offer him a cup of coffee. I hear myself saying in Afrikaans, *Wil jy koffie hê?*

The burglar always accepts and lowers his gun. I even turn my back on the intruder to boil the kettle. My hands tighten their grip on the steering wheel as I imagine the scene.

We sit down at the table my father made for Ruth a week after they got married, drinking coffee out of porcelain mugs. After my initial greeting in Afrikaans we speak in English, because I can control my emotions in my father's tongue.

In this daymare I accidentally activate the secret alarm to my security company. They arrive with guns in hand and I tell them that my cat tripped the alarm. The burglar looks on calmly. The security men leave. The burglar pulls the index finger of his left hand across his throat in that universal sign language for *your time is up, buddy.* With his right hand, he traces a star on his forehead. I watch as the bullet travels towards me. It enters my body, and I slide out of the frame.

There is no satisfying equivalent in my mother tongue for the term *random events.*

I am a random event, directionless, waiting for a place to happen.

I roam my mind searching for neutral ground. A car is hooting behind me. I have stopped at a green robot.

Ruth

"Look at me!" the girlchild shouts, "Look at me!" Ruth smiles, looking at a young mother in the park opposite the café, pushing her child on a swing. The child arches her body backwards, holding tightly onto the chains that anchor the wooden seat to the metal frame. Her hair forms a stroke of light against the sky. The girlchild kicks higher and higher with her short legs.

She remembers Gloria on a bench in a park, the winterfawn wisteria branches behind her mother revealing the illicit smokers – young boys with greasy hair and mean mouths who frightened Ruth. During the summer months their laughter was clouded in smoke, hidden behind the green hedge, heavy with purple racemes.

Other mothers huddled inside their kitchens, warm loaves emerging from hot ovens, while Ruth called to her mother, her legs swinging higher, higher, in a dizzying rhythm, "Look at me . . . look at me!"

Her mother took a tartan-patterned flask from the basket next to her. The hot liquid steamed as she unscrewed the lid, and poured a cup.

As they prepared for their trip to the park, Ruth watched her mother tip the whisky from the bottle into the coffee.

"God it's cold out there!" Gloria said, tightening the cap of the flask, pushing past Frankie and bending down to button Ruth's coat. "You take her out one day, feel for yourself!"

Swinging high, Ruth looked at the snow gullied up in the mountains across the bay, too far to reach and touch. Picture snow on a Christmas card.

Gloria leaned back against the wooden slats of the bench with closed eyes.

Back home, Ruth played with wooden spools filled with fine satin thread. Gloria stitched rows of colours onto satin, mother of Ruth, doing what mothers do.

Frankie muttered, "Where do you think the money for this finery comes from?" He knocked the spools from the sewing table, saying, "It's not as if you ever make anything anyone can use."

He threw the red dresses onto the floor – knitted one after the other, too wide around the waist for Gloria, who continued to grow thinner, and thinner. Next day he came home again with spooled thread tumbling from his pockets.

"Never enough," he said, "Nothing I do is ever enough. Now see what you made me do."

Gloria's neck, tilted back to the weak sun, looked like a frail stalk holding a heavy flower. Ruth kicked her legs in protest when Gloria grabbed the chains of the swing, and pulled her from the seat.

"Come Ruth, let's go home! Let's go and paint the door of our house green! Heart-of-the-forest-green, my little jelly bean!" Ruth laughed at this, "Silly mommy," she said, skipping next to Gloria, "Silly-billy mommy!"

Later that day, Frankie passed through the door.

"And what the hell is the meaning of this?"

Green stickiness furred the white cotton of his shirt.

"Nothing," Gloria said, "Just a green door I felt like having, a green door."

Ruth hands a loaf of bread to the *bergie* woman, who squats next to the entrance of the shop. A field of green spins behind her eyelids as she walks the short distance home.

Inside, she puts the packet of yeast on the table. The cream-coloured mixing bowl is ready and waiting.

Morgan

An hour and a half later I have cleared the stray weeds from the labyrinth pathways. My skin feels prickly from the heat and sweat. I attach the sprinkler head to the hosepipe and hang it upside down over the branch of a tree, open the tap, and, after peeling off my jeans, T-shirt and panties, I step into the makeshift outdoor shower. With the open palm of my hand I press my belly, grateful that I can't feel any evidence of the baby growing inside.

"You can't be serious," Timo had said yesterday, when I told him I was considering an abortion.

"I didn't plan this," I answered, "It's the worst possible time, everything in Scotland will be so much more complicated with a baby."

"Or not," he said, "It'll give me something to do, we'll manage."

His generous, loving response infuriated me.

"Easy for you to say, you are not going to swell up like a balloon and leak milk from cracked nipples, not to mention giving birth."

Timo took his arm away from under my head, and got up from the bed. "I can't tell you what to do," he said. "But know that I will be very disappointed, devastated, if you choose to abort our baby. Just tell me before you do. Promise me I won't come home one evening to find out that you've gone ahead and done it."

I turned on my side so that he couldn't see my eyes, which had filled with tears.

"Promise," he said, touching my shoulder.

"I promise," I said into the pillow. "I have two more weeks to decide."

Fat raindrops join the spray of water from the hosepipe. I stand with eyes closed and arms thrown wide, enjoying the sensation on my skin.

I phoned Isabel, after I had cleared the labyrinth, overcome by a need to tell her of the baby. Standing on top of the highest hill on the farm, talking to her, I saw the dark storm clouds gather around the church tower and heard thunder rumble in the distance. Thunder and lightning are uncommon phenomena in these parts, and the dogs in the town below will soon be howling in distress.

A flash of lightning sends me running to the house, and into the bathroom where I dry off, and dress. It'll have to be Plan B, I decide, dinner inside, in the dining room, and not outside under the camphor tree.

I open the drawers of the faded blue kitchen dresser. Inside them is a jumble of cutlery, cast-offs from several generations. I count out six bone-handled knives, six matching forks and six spoons. Ruth is sure to bring dessert – she knows I have a sweet tooth.

From the shelves behind the glass-fronted doors I take six plates, each one with a different pattern. And six side plates, and six dessert bowls. I count out six embroidered napkins – embroidered linen squares with a twisting line of ivy leaves. I carry them to the table, which is covered with the pumpkin-orange cotton cloth that was once my bedspread at home.

Tafeldektyd! my mother would call, reminding me to set the table for supper.

The glasses are opaque with dust, and I fill the sink with hot soapy water to wash them. Washing dishes is the only domestic chore I enjoy. Doing it slowly, it becomes a meditation. One glass at a time, then rinse and dry with a clean cloth. Placed on the table, they shine and sparkle in the fading light of the kitchen.

But something is missing. Although the centre of the table will soon be filled with plates of food, it looks empty; too bare. My grandmother would place flowers in a bowl in the centre, if this were her table. My mother would do something unexpected, and possibly sentimental, like placing the plates on large red paper hearts. I throw my raincoat over my shoulders and walk outside to fetch six white stones from my grandfather's cairn. Back inside I dry them and write a name on each with my mother's silver pen.

"Everybody should have a silver pen," she once told me, as she slipped it into the cutlery drawer, among the knives and forks, "Much more useful than sliced bread."

I place the stones on top of Gloria's napkins.

Isabel, Ruth, Gloria, Jonathan, Timo, Morgan.

Perfect.

Isabel

I take a shortcut over the mountain on Redhill Road. Fire devastation is visible everywhere. The sea falls behind me as I clear the ridge and drive towards the highway that will lead me to Morgan's roses. My mother is back in the car, again asking questions, one after the other, not waiting for answers.

"Is language the monster under your childhood bed, with the power of re-forming the man that ripped out your tongue? Do you fear that he might suddenly appear in a shiny black dress suit with coattails and top hat? Smelling of XXX-mints and mincemeat-on-toast?"

I curl my tongue back in my mouth so that the words that could call him back to life cannot escape. I see his sad smile hovering over my mouth as I glance in the rear-view mirror.

I was his *kleinkind lieflingskind*. Grandchild, darlingchild.

A battered copy of one of Gloria's knitting patterns lies at the bottom of my handbag where it is slowly disintegrating. She scribbled words and sentences in the margins of the patterns; *I lie to live to lie. The snailpath curls forever. Rusty keys don't turn.*

It reminds me of the rotting Bible I once found in the storeroom in the back yard of my grandparents' house. It was the day of Frankie's funeral. I refused to go to the church, or graveyard, and stayed behind instead. Ruth left me in charge of getting tea ready for everybody. I was alone in my grandfather's house and started walking down the passage to his bedroom, and the drawer that held the box. On the threshold to the room, I turned and ran into the sunlight outside, to the old abandoned outside toilet, which had become a storeroom for trash over the years. A Gloria grimescene.

Among bits of mangled steel and broken glass I found an old musty Bible. Damp and buried, the pages stuck together. Strangely, it did not feel like a treasure – and I knew enough about Bibles to realise that this was no way to treat them at all. My heart beat guiltily as I pulled it out from under a rusty kitchen chair. Had I perhaps thrown it there, when no one was looking? When even I wasn't looking?

It smelt like something that had died a long time ago.

What kind of a person would throw a Bible away? Definitely not someone my father would approve of. I tore out a clump of sticky pages and smoothed it down. The dress that Ruth made me wear that day had no pockets, nowhere to hide treasures, so I flattened it between my belly and the front of my panties.

Once home, I separated the pages carefully and started writing my own Bible. I still have my hand-written toilet-trash Bible, and it starts with a poem about Frankie's funeral.

wet bible in the backyard trash
dust to dust
mould grew on it like a furry coat
turning leather to rust.

For a long time I imagined this was the most beautiful poem ever written. I was ten years old and imagined all kinds of things, as my mother was fond of reminding me.

Liar, liar, pants on fire.

This time of year I suffer from hayfever. My eyes water all the time, streaking my cheeks with salt. I am driving down the highway, autopiloting, hoping I'm not too late to find yellow roses for Morgan. Germiston Gold, maybe. This was the first rose David had planted for Ruth in McGregor. Homecoming yellow for a farewell.

And tonight, four generations of women will gather under one roof. Gloria, Ruth, Morgan and Isabel. GRMI, GIRM. IRGM. MIRG. RIGM. The word refuses to form itself into an anagram. It remains stuck, becomes the sound of a throat clearing. Then, as my mind leaps to Jonathan, I think of *grim*. At the farewell tonight in McGregor we will all meet on neutral ground, everybody in this family moving, or about to move.

I change back into third gear and overtake a slow Toyota. I imagine the shape of a fifteen-year old Morgan in the passenger seat, and I hear her voice.

"A flower in which all four whorls are present is said to be a complete flower. If any of the non-essential whorls is not present the flower is incomplete."

"Is a whorl a petal?"

"When you say it, it sounds funny. *Whorl*. Like a . . . you know . . . prostitute."

"Well. Don't blame me, blame the English language."

"A *whirl* is not a petal, but one of the *whirls* that form a flower is made up by petals. That *whirl* is called the corolla."

"Like Toyota Corolla?"

The drivers of Toyotas seem especially peaceful people, with an unhurried approach to life. I often get stuck behind them in traffic – and don't feel so kindly then.

My mind hops like the sand flies I saw on the beach this morning. It settles on a conversation with my mother. "You are my miracle," she told me when she found me with my dead brother's umbilical cord in my hand. "You were not supposed to happen."

For days I walked around with this rope of words hanging down my throat, *notsupposedtohappen*. Where would I be if I never happened? How does one happen? I thought of the blood-filled scales filled with empty bubbles, *molecules*, this new word I had found in my dictionary – strong and powerful.

Light drizzle coats my hair as I get out of the car at Chart Farm and walk towards the counter to fetch secateurs and a basket. As I walk towards the roses everything seems clear and simple for the briefest of moments.

Last week when I visited Gloria at Ruth's request, my grandmother grabbed at me, as is her habit – always snaring those who pass her by. She said: "Help me to die, Isa. I know you want me dead. I'm asking you for a kindness, not a killing."

Trying to pull my arm free, I thought, *nothing grand about this grim-mother, grabmother, grubmother.* Gloria had almost fallen – making me feel I had committed a deliberate act of violence. The fantasy of my youth, my childhood, made real.

More gently, I removed her hand – this time there was no resistance – and said, *"Moenie nonsens praat nie."* I spoke Afrikaans simply because Gloria hates it whenever I do. All her life Gloria has aspired to the other side. The more glamorous, English side. She sympathised with official attempts to outlaw the use of Afrikaans in schools, and applauded the handing out of dunce caps to the unfortunate speakers of the new upstart language.

The only time she was truly proud of her daughter, was when Ruth married David, son of Scottish immigrants. She took it for granted that I would marry an Englishman. And fate handed me one, not the *boerseun* I had hoped for. Gloria got her wish.

"I am not talking nonsense," Gloria said, "Just slip something into my drink. Don't tell me when. Just make it soon."

"Liewe Here, Ouma," was my reply, shaking my head like Ruth did.

I place the first rose in the basket, and see a bath filled with petals, in my grandmother's house. Frankie had been dead for a month, and Gloria had pulled all the dead petals from the funeral flowers, and put them in the bath. My mother and I arrived with a meal for her, calling down the passage as we entered the kitchen.

"Go look for her," my mother instructed, "I'll start heating up the food."

I walked towards the sound of splashing water, calling. My grandmother emerged from the bathroom. Dead rose petals stuck to her naked, damp skin. She walked towards me and grabbed my arm to steady her. The large pores on her nose were clogged with face powder, and she smelled of something sour and sharp. I wanted to pull away but my grandmother's grip was firm. Her left eye was watery and shiny, like the black olives in the green bowl in the kitchen that Ruth liked to eat while cooking.

I didn't want to look at her, and tried to focus instead on the remaining petals in the bath behind her. Gloria pushed my head down towards her drooping breasts and said, "This is what happens to you when you grow old."

Her breasts, cupped by her bony hands, accused me of something I couldn't yet name. Only much later did I understand.

I stood accused of the youth that Frankie had found so irresistible.

The basket is full of yellow, orange, and pink roses. Their smell releases a memory of being pushed down a passage, strapped into a pram. I remember the dark door that beckoned at the end, remember straining against the straps to follow my mother as she entered through the open door.

I saw Gloria, facedown, her blouse buttons undone, as if she had tried to tear it from her body. Vomit was matted into her hair, and Ruth rushed to her mother's side. I heard my mother's

175

angry voice screaming, and heard myself crying as if the voice came from under the bed in my grandmother's bedroom, where an empty bottle gave a glassy wink. Pills lay scattered like coloured sweeties all over the carpet.

I watched as Ruth scooped bits of food from Gloria's mouth and forced sips of water into her slack mouth, which drained into the powdery folds of my grandmother's neck. My mother leaned her back against the edge of the bed with Gloria a birdwing weight on her lap, and I stopped crying. Silence floated into the room like a thick fog. The tuberoses on Gloria's bedside table released their scent of peppermint and roses into the room.

I turn to the right, up the narrow path that takes me into the heart of the rose garden, looking for one last perfect flower. Their abundant beauty surrounds me, in all the colours one can imagine, with a fine spray of soft rain deepening their brilliance.

How can I even think of killing my grandmother on a day like this? And yet, why not? More like a belated assisted suicide anyway – and I may just be able to live with that.

I pay for the roses and convince the woman behind the counter to lend me a bucket with water so that they will keep fresh in the car. The rain has stopped and the sun is warming the day.

With the bucket wedged tightly behind my seat, I drive off towards Ruth's flat. My cellphone rings. Morgan. Her voice sounds strange, but it could just be the phone reception.

"Hi Mom. I want to check about tonight? Timo is bringing Dad, no need to have both your cars here tonight . . . could you please bring some candles? They only stock the fancy ones here, those twisty ones like ice-cream cones."

"And only red ones, I suppose!"

"Exactly . . . Mom . . . could you . . . a little bit earlier . . . it would be . . . something to tell . . . "

The mountains surrounding the farmhouse are a barrier to cellphone reception, and Isabel imagines Morgan twisting and turning in a circle, on the highest outcrop of rock outside the house, trying to get better reception.

"Morgan? I'm losing you, you're breaking up . . . see you later!"

I feel funny talking into thin air while driving. Not yet used to the hands-free phone kit. No more distinguishing between ordinary nut-cakes and working people clinching a deal and having a conversation. Talking out loud while driving has received the official seal of approval.

*

Carrying the bucket of roses, I enter my mother's kitchen. Ruth is busy making a pot of tea.

"I thought it best to get them out of the sun," I offer as an answer to Ruth's frown. The dirty plastic bucket looks out of place in the sparkling clean kitchen.

"Have you been baking?" I ask, sniffing the air.

"And what if I have?"

Once more I am a child in my mother's kitchen. I lean back against the black granite counter-top, facing Ruth. A vase filled with overblown poppies reflects into its dark surface, dusted with turmeric pollen. I lift one of the flowers from the vase and twirl its stem between my fingers.

"Do you know all the different functions of the stem of a flower?" I ask.

"I never thought about it," Ruth replies, "Is it something I should know?"

"Well, let me see if I can remember this biology lesson from Morgan. Remember how she used to entertain me on the way to school?"

My mother shrugs and places the cups on a tray.

"Let me see . . . the stem bears leaves in the most favourable position for light and air, it bears flowers in the most favourable position for pollination, it bears the fruit and seeds in the best position for dispersal, and stores food that isn't needed by the plant at the time. And then something about strengthening tissue and vascular tissue, which always made me think of flower stems as thin green muscles."

"You're thinking of xylem, the hard part of the vascular bundle that carries water and minerals from the roots to the rest of the plant."

"I knew I could trust you to know the facts after all!" I say, pushing away from the counter and taking the tray from her.

The kitchen is not big enough for a table, but Ruth still prepares her meals with the same care, even though she now eats off a pale wooden tray, seated in front of the television. She will never admit this to Isabel, though, and pretends that she uses the small table pushed against the only wall with a window.

At night she reads herself to sleep, opening the books at the red-flagged familiars and savouring a three-course meal while sipping a glass of warm vanilla milk.

"Do you mind if I have a quick look at this?" I take the yellow-spined recipe book from the row on the counter, and place it on the tray. We walk to the living room and sit down.

"I see you've unpacked all the boxes," I say, opening the book at a green marker.

"It's taken me long enough, I started missing things I needed." She passes me a cup of tea.

"Thanks, you still make the best cup of tea. Mom, tell me, why on earth did I leave the planning for tonight so late? Hmmm – just listen to this . . . Beetroot and Orange Soup: 4-5 beetroot, peeled and grated; 1 tbsp salt; 1 tsp dried thyme; half tsp pepper; 1 bayleaf; 6 cups water, 2 cups canned tomato juice; 1 cup orange juice, 2 tbsp gelatine . . . sounds delicious."

Ruth takes the book from me and puts it on the couch next to her.

"Well, you could have asked me to do the cooking, you know that. I wanted to make lamb with parsley sauce, my butcher always has very sweet neck chops, and for dessert I thought a mocha torte with ladyfingers . . . Morgan would have loved that."

"You keep forgetting that we're vegetarian! None of us eat meat. I can't think of anything more disgusting than eating the neck of a lamb."

"Oh well, I'm tired," says Ruth, turning away. "And all these goodbyes make me even more tired."

"Have you been to the farm since Dad died?"

"You would know if I had, wouldn't you?"

I ignore this slight belligerence, evident in my mother ever since my arrival.

"At my age, every goodbye could be a last goodbye." Ruth complains.

"Gloria is still alive," I say.

But this is not what my mother wants to hear.

"Jonathan understands. He brought me those flowers in the kitchen last week and we had a nice chat. Their heads were still closed and they looked quite obscenely like hairy testicles on fresh green stalks."

Ruth starts telling me, again, about her last visit to the farm, during the time that David spent a month there with Morgan. It was then that he told her he would not be going back; that he wanted to spend the remaining years of his life alone. To feel what that feels like, alone with God.

Lately, Ruth spends a lot of time re-telling old stories. Just to make sure I get the facts right. The truth is important to her; my mother tolerates no lies.

One morning, she tells me now, she walked down the mountain path into the village of McGregor to buy milk and a newspaper. She passed a field, yellow with oxalis. The rustling sound of dark-leafed apricot trees filled her ears. She noticed a strange pattern on the grass and, walking closer, she saw it was thin trails of blood. It was only then that she saw the castrated bullocks standing listlessly in the sun, their blood-smeared hind legs covered with flies.

Next to the *leiwater* trough, which fed rivulets of water down the rows of apricot trees, was a neat row of testicles. They glistened in the early morning sun. Through the outer transparent membrane Ruth could see the looping patterning of veins. Mesmerised, she continued to stare, ignoring the blood-iron smell in the air.

"What is it about blood that makes us stop and stare?" I ask, and my mother shakes her head.

"I don't know. After Davey's stillbirth I felt that I had had my fill of blood . . . it was before the time of sonars and scans, you know. My doctor said he couldn't detect a heartbeat when I told him I didn't feel any movement. It was in the thirty-eighth week. I kept hoping, though."

When her labour pains started my mother thought she was going to die. He was a large baby with broad shoulders. After his head emerged, with a peaceful angel-face, as David later told her, she lost the will to push, and the baby remained stuck.

She heard the doctor swear softly under his breath as he reached in and snapped the sapling collarbone to pull the baby out. With David at her side, Ruth said goodbye to this small person she would never know, but loved already, since love happens on a cellular level, seeps in through the blood, quickening with each heartbeat. When Ruth asked to keep a bit of the umbilical cord no one argued with her. The doctor was efficient and polite.

"Like an undertaker," Ruth says. Her left hand strays to the book next to her, and her fingers play with the red and green flagged markers.

"Gloria said that just as she had killed her mother, I'd killed my son. She seemed to appreciate the symmetry."

They kept his ashes in a jar until after my birth. Only then did David and Ruth feel ready to release him.

Davey's ashes were scattered in McGregor, under the aloe bush next to the back door. In time Ruth forgot what she did with the bit of umbilical cord, forgot that she kept it in an envelope where it lay in her bottom drawer among old baby clothes. That is where I found it, years later, when I was ten or eleven. By then, Frankie had died. Ruth found me, sitting on her bed and staring at the stumpy bit of dried flesh, weightless on my upturned palm. The envelope with Davey's name on was lying next to me. I was about to hear Davey's story for the first time.

"What is this . . . it looks disgusting. And who is Davey?" I asked.

Ruth gave me the truth.

"It is a dried up bit of umbilical cord. It is the bit that remains attached to the baby after the birth. The rest of the cord is attached to the afterbirth, which is expelled from the womb with a few powerful contractions, right at the end. It sort of slips out."

She said this while taking the scrap of flesh from my palm, and wrapped it once more in the tissue paper square. I hoped the look on my face made it clear that I already knew more than I needed to know. And less.

"But I still don't know who Davey is," I nevertheless said.

And that was how the first telling happened, of the stillborn brother and Ruth's still sadness and how she never wanted me to grow up thinking that I was a mere replacement. My mother told me about her swollen breasts and expressing milk with a

181

glass and rubber contraption to avoid inflammation of the milk ducts. She spoke in clear, scientific terms, avoiding ambiguity at any cost.

Using the proper words separates meaning from feeling; it keeps emotions under control.

I listened with my head to one side, Bible-listening style, wanting to touch Ruth but not daring to.

Just a stroke of her arm, maybe. But Ruth's back was very straight and her eyes very bright and I felt powerless and somehow ashamed. I decided to ask a practical question.

"What did you do with all the milk?"

"Oh . . . I gave it to the hospital. There were many women who didn't produce enough milk for their babies. But I overflowed."

"Maybe you were crying milk, not tears."

The brightness in my mother's eyes spilled over. We sat side by side on the bed and cried for lost firstborn, lost brother. Later that day we buried the cord under the lemon tree in the back garden.

Davey has two burial sites, one fragrant, one bitter.

Lost and found and buried twice.

*

Back in the kitchen I outline a pattern in the dusting of orange pollen with my left index finger. A spiral growing outward. Ruth lifts my hand and wipes the counter with a damp cloth.

"You're not still drawing in dust, are you?" she asks, handing me a cup to pack away. I notice how sparse my mother's hair has become. Her scalp gleams through in places; the springy coarseness has gone. Her head resembles that of a fondly remembered childhood doll whose hair I once cut on impulse and in anger one Sunday morning in my wooden house. I cried as I washed the tufted scalp. Until that moment I hadn't questioned the life-like quality of the doll's hair, and felt betrayed by the neat rows of stitching across the flesh-coloured plastic. The doll was exposed as a fraud.

My wooden playhouse stood in the cement courtyard just outside my mother's kitchen. It didn't have any real furniture, only bright cushions and a low table with paper and finger paints, as well as dolls and a box of dress-up clothes. Whenever I got bored sitting on Ruth's table, watching her cook, I slid off and walked outside through the back door to this playhouse. Before entering I gave my mother a little wave through the kitchen window. Ruth waited, floury hand raised, to return it. Then, with a flash of white apron, she turned around and continued her baking.

From inside this dark cushioned space I looked at the sunny rectangle of world outside, my legs drawn up against my chest, my hands linked over my knees. I sat like that for a long time, counting the number of flies that passed by the door, or imagining the taste of the food Ruth was preparing. It was easy to know what something would taste like, simply by smelling it.

Sometimes I ran into the kitchen, pinching my nose to trap the smell, and hopped up and down in front of my mother, open-mouthed, making urgent, bird-like noises. It was the only way to test if I had managed to match a smell with its taste. Ruth indulged me, and spooned the food onto my impatient tongue.

One day I slid from the flour-covered table just as my mother was bending down to put two cakes into the hot oven.

"Careful!" Ruth said, as I knocked over a jug of water standing near the edge of the table.

"Sorry!" My voice shrank with guilt. Ruth said nothing, just walked over with a cloth to mop up the water. Her glasses were steamed up from the hot oven, and her mouth disappeared into her face, leaving only a line.

I looked up into her opaque stare, repeating how sorry I was, over and over, waiting to be pardoned. Not yet knowing that it was my need for forgiveness that scoured my mother's nerves raw.

Not the spilling, not the mess.

I wanted something from her that Ruth was not prepared to give; that she had run out of. She was an empty sack of flour, because Gloria had used up the entire supply. My need for forgiveness set Ruth's jaw like a clamp.

My mother's forgiveness felt like shortbread pastry rubbed between fingers, I could already taste its sweetness in my mouth, but the best she could do was force a smile as she pushed me towards the door.

"It's okay, Isabel. Go outside and play."

Gloria arrived for a visit most days, and I watched from inside my playhouse as my grandmother's stick legs appeared alongside my mother's plump calves, a lopsided four-legged beast passing my door. I hid under a pile of cushions until I was sure they were inside the house.

I touch my mother briefly on her shoulder where she stands at the sink, rinsing yellow pollen from the cloth.

"Jonathan was offered a lift by Timo. I think Morgan wants the two of them to get to know each other a little better."

"Do you think it's serious? Between Timo and Morgan?"

"Who knows . . . I don't think about it any more. Will you be okay driving yourself and Gloria?"

"Of course. I've always done the driving, know that road like the back of my hand. He wasn't much help with things like that."

Ruth smoothes the wrung cloth over the edge of the basin and leans over to close the kitchen window.

"Actually, Mom, you've always done exactly what you wanted . . . always had your own way. Stop pretending self-pity."

My knife is so very sharp. Dare I add love?

Ruth turns round, startled by the challenge.

"Have I? Always had my own way?"

I hold my mother's eyes with mine, and in the stillness, disturbed by the humming of the fridge, the smell of peppermint wafts past.

It is lifted on the breeze from the pot on the windowsill.

Ruth's mouth tightens, a thin line across her face, that familiar line I fear to cross.

Liar, liar, pants on fire, your nose is as long as a telephone wire.

*

I get into the car with the wine in a box on the back seat and drive away from Ruth's flat. The roses are back behind the seat. I stop at the red light at the bottom of Ruth's street. Looking left, I can see an empty child's swing in the small park, swaying from metal chains. Two mothers are talking, with babies on their hips, leaning against its metal frame. My childhood swing is long abandoned; I can no longer fly off into the blue.

I think of the cloth in Ruth's kitchen, smoothed over the edge of the sink, a dishrag, with no other purpose in life but to wipe and to clean. I feel responsible for the pollen stain; my drawing caused it.

Ruth avoided my eyes when she handed me the box of wine – its bulk an excuse to keep us at arm's length from each other.

"See you later, then," she said, as she helped me with the bucket of roses, pushing their stems deeper into the water. "I don't think they'll last till tonight," she added, and walked back to her flat.

Blue scum laced the high-tide mark on the beach yesterday morning, made up of small blue octopus creatures, bluebottles, and tiny bluepurple snails with bubble bodies. As it did this morning, kelp foam glided like hovercraft over the wet sand. It was a study in blues and purples under a pink dome of sky.

The blue of the morning stirred a memory: I was four, and Ruth had taken me for a walk on the beach. We were bent low, examining tiny sea animals. Ruth's fingers were prodding and pointing out the diversity of patterns and designs. My mother's sense of wonder was contagious, and I talked along excitedly.

A shadow fell over us and I looked up to see a stranger, long hair windcoiled like seaweed around her face and throat. She said, "Look out for the blue cat, I think you will like it," then got up and walked off with a little wave. It was a child's wave – a rapid bending of four fingers onto her palm; down, up, down – and then she was gone.

"What did she say to you?" Ruth asked, for the wind had blown the words past her ears and into mine. I hesitated to answer her. I found it hard to believe that a blue cat existed, and realised for the first time in my life that adults can also tell lies. It didn't matter that I found a small blue plastic cat just a short time later, where the woman must have known we would bend down for the shells around it.

I picked up the blue plastic cat and put it in my box of treasures at home, where I also kept marbles and shells and my collection of plastic ballerinas. The ones with gold and silver skirts and pointy feet were my passion for years.

Ruth stuck their feet into the icing of my birthday cakes. They stood frozen and silent in their frosted sugar field. For me, the best moment was when I could lick the ballerina feet after the last child had gone home and I was alone in the kitchen. With eyes closed I licked each pointy foot completely clean, until no trace of sweetness was left.

My father disapproved of the ballerinas. I heard Ruth say to him, one evening while icing the cake, "You forbid her to go to the ballet class, which is bad enough, just let her have this. She loves the idea of dancing."

"But it's sinful. To flaunt your body like that. Who knows what ideas she could get from it?"

"She is four years old, David. Just let her be."

The next time I licked sweetness from the foot of a ballerina I wondered what it was that made them so sinful. So full of sin. Sin was red, and felt like a strangled tightness, like when I buckled my shoes. I knew it had something to do with the church David went to every Sunday. Ruth always said goodbye to him at the door, still in slippers and dressing gown.

Years later, I added something else to my collection in the box. I slid it underneath the ballerinas. It was a drawing Gloria had made of me when I was two years old.

"By the time you were born, I was out of practice," Gloria told me, "But you can have it anyway. I have no use for it."

I couldn't understand the nervousness I felt then, and fear, as I took the drawing from her. I hated the idea of my grandmother fixing her gaze on me – a moth trapped in the spider's web.

I drive past the first wall Morgan ever built. It is next to a road I travel often. A beautiful sandstone wall that will outlive us all.

The first time I saw it, I wanted to catch something of myself in that wall, in the careful placing of stone upon stone, but I was nowhere to be found. Morgan is so purely *herself* that it hurts. Or rather, it hurts that I see Jonathan in that wall, see his bent head over a pile of seeds, carefully sorting and classifying.

Gloria

Gloria notices the red light flashing at her front door, which indicates that someone is pressing the doorbell. Somewhat unsteadily, she walks down the short passage, after the long sit on her bed. Through the peephole she sees Ruth's fishbowl face. Unlatching the security chain, she opens the door.

"Have you been sleeping?" Ruth demands to know, eyes scanning the room with habitual nervousness for signs of drunken disorder. After 76 years of mothering mother she feels entitled to abandon pleasantries. No more hugs or kisses or how are you? The last time Ruth tried to hug Gloria, she complained that it hurt her ribs.

"Didn't sleep much last night. You know how he snores. Kept me up all night. Did Morgan land safely? Did you bring me some wedding cake?"

How nice to live in such a befuddled world, Ruth thinks. Though not much of life makes sense anyway, even before senile dementia sets in.

"No Mom, The party is only happening tonight. I'll be driving us to the farm. Last minute change of plans. I saw Isabel a while ago and Jonathan won't be picking us up anymore."

"The farm? What farm?"

"Ours. In McGregor. With the olive trees and the apricots. Remember? We were there last Christmas."

"We had an ugly thorn tree branch for a Christmas tree. Morgan's idea of an African Christmas. So you didn't bring me cake?"

Gloria's constant craving for sweet foods maddens Ruth – she is like a needy baby who can't get enough of her mother's breast, who grabs at it in shopping queues, on a bus, anywhere.

"No Mom, no cake. There will be lots tonight, though. Come on, I must help you get ready. I want to leave no later than three. It is now just after one. What did you have for breakfast? Has the nurse been in to check on you?"

"How would I know? I was sleeping. I haven't eaten. I'm not hungry."

Ruth leads Gloria towards the couch in her sitting room.

"Well, I brought you some papino and strawberries. Sit down, I'll make us some lunch. Be a good girl, and you can have some sweets afterwards. I brought your favourite kind."

In the kitchen Ruth finds a pile of cut beans on the table, leaking green juice into the wood. She turns to find a bowl to put them in; as she bends down, her face reflects in the glass oven door. A child with plump unbaked features is reflected next to her, also peering through the glass-fronted oven door. Her eyes are raisins pressed in cookie dough. She is crying, and licking the salty tears from her cheeks.

Together, they watch as a hand slides out a grey baking tray filled with gingerbread men, all melted together into a many-headed monster.

Isabel

I pull onto the shoulder of the road and stop the car in the shade of a flyover bridge. From the cubbyhole I take a dog-eared journal, which I keep to ease me through the word attacks that pounce whenever I am driving.

The red spine of the journal opens at a poem from a long time ago.

Division takes place within the parent envelope
and each daughter cell forms for itself
a new cell wall.
The original envelope
– stretched in this way –
absorbs more and more water until
towards the exterior
it gradually shades off
into the surrounding liquid.

I close my eyes to enter the velvet world of lichen and fungus and moss. Whiplash filaments and other unexpected word gifts. A stray sentence enters my head: *No intercellular air spaces occur between the adjacent cells.* It all made perfect sense to me then. Not any more. Whatever magic I once used to turn dry botanical descriptions into poetry, to momentarily lose the path to the familiar meaning of words, is lost forever.

Elephant Eye Mountain lies to my right. We passed it every morning on our way to school, Morgan pointing and announcing the emotional state of the mountain.

"Look!" she would say, "The elephant is weeping today."

Looking up at the cave set high in the elephant-shaped mountain I see that it is shrouded with cloud. I shift upright into my seat and start the car again. As I pull away into the stream of traffic I remember those moments of perfect agreement between my daughter and me.

I am sick of waiting for Morgan to leave. Cooking, walking, driving the car, shopping, talking, gardening – it's all just waiting for the pre-destined moment when I will watch my daughter walk through the metal detectors at the airport, her rucksack swallowed by the rubber-fringed mouth of the conveyer belt. She will turn back only once, and wave a small wave. I will watch her walk away until I can no longer see her.

The ribbon road unfurls in front of me, the car fragrant with yellow roses. I see myself stumble and fall. I am lying on the polished kitchen floor, and my mother, who is looking like a warrior, holds a sharp knife in her hand. She seems to offer the knife to me, pointing the blade tip straight at me. Cold spreads through my belly. Next to my reflection in the polished floor is that of a child, a girl with wild frozen hair. Her eyes are closed, her eyelids a bruised purple. I put my hand on the child's hand and feel the heat enter my body. A thousand tiny fishes are tugging at the inside of my belly, mouths open and sucking. I push my arms straight against the steering wheel, pressing my back deep into the leather seat of the car, banishing the frozen child.

The smell of leather and roses is reality, I tell myself. This is real. This is my life.

But nothing is real unless you imagine it to be so.

I want to be somewhere, and waiting isn't getting me anywhere.

"I want to be somewhere and waiting isn't getting me anywhere." Saying the words out loud makes them sound wrong, like one of those spot-the-mistake-sentences from primary school. *I'm not going nowhere.*

A red robot stops the car – the one at the flower-sellers who never have any roses. They have arums and Barberton daisies and irises and proteas. Pincushions, and even a few pots filled with West Coast vygies. *Mesembs. Besems. Brooms.* I try to imagine their root systems, trained by my daughter to be aware of what develops under the soil where the eye cannot see. Root caps, and root hairs, growing points and regions of elongation.

"The tip of the root is covered by a cap shaped like a thimble to protect it from injury and damage . . . the root cap cells become slimy, thus reducing friction between cap and soil particles. Worn-out root cap cells are replaced by new ones."

I turn into the parking lot of the shopping centre where all my culinary dreams will come true.

Suffocating in the memory-laden air, I open the back door and lean over to cover the roses with newspaper. On my way here I passed the old turn-off to Morgan's school, the slipway that leads past Victoria Hospital, where the sick and the bandaged often stand chatting on the sidewalk in open-backed hospital gowns. As a child I called this feeling rising now in my breast *closetphobic.*

Sometimes I would ask my daughter, "Do you ever get tired of learning facts? Don't you sometimes wish you could make up stuff about plants and flowers and animals?"

"What would be the point of that?" was Morgan's sensible reply.

I push a trolley down the well-lit aisles of a Pick 'n Pay food hall. A great weariness comes over me the second my hands connect with the handle of a shopping trolley. My mind goes blank as I place random items into the trolley. This morning's planning feels futile, and I move on instinct, throw in bread, cheese, ham. Put back the ham when I remember we have all become vegetarian over the last couple of months. I miss ham and mustard on fresh white bread, but will never admit that to my mother. Even Jonathan has given up eating meat – and he found my surprise at that insulting.

Fruit, yoghurt, salad. The trolley is getting full and still I have no idea what I want to make for this special supper.

Gloria

"I'm going to lie down for a minute," Gloria says, adding a cup to the pile of dishes Ruth is taking to the kitchen.

"I'll settle you in the chair over there. In the sun. Do you want a blanket?"

Gloria brushes Ruth's attempt away.

"I'll get what I need. You can just carry on with the dishes. You have always been a good girl."

Ruth watches as her mother walks down the short passage to her bedroom. She calls to Gloria's stooped back covered with her lilac cardigan, "Let me know if I can help you with anything! We have to leave in just over an hour. I'll wake you up if you fall asleep."

No answer, just a weary lifting of Gloria's right arm, a dismissive acknowledgement. Typical, Ruth thinks. She knows I exist, but it makes no difference to her life. Some things never change.

Ruth starts to wash the pile of dirty dishes in the sink, thinks of Isabel's *grimescene*. Her hands sunk deep into the warm suds she washes the dishes, one item at a time. Two bowls, two plates, two knives, two forks.

Gloria sits on the bed, on Frankie's side. She opens the top drawer of the small cabinet next to the bed – for the first time in over forty years. The smell of peppermint still lingers. Frankie liked his mouth to smell fresh, always.

"For the girls," he used to say. She tugs at the loose section of wood at the back of the drawer and reaches inside for the small parcel she hid there after his funeral. Taking it out, she removes the thick rubber cross holding the contents together.

Gloria pulls the metal wastebasket closer and drops the stacked photographs into it, one by one. Neatly labelled photographs with codes written in each corner: G6MBB, B1YBB, G5YRB.

The familiar faces of these children haunt her. She can even remember some of their names.

Susan, Thomas, Anna, Francis.

She feels the stub of charcoal between her fingers, and sees the whiteness of a blank page. Remembers Ruthie's soft body on a blanket in the sun.

Frankie explained that the codes referred to the physical attributes of the child in each photograph. The numbers were the child's age, and G or B referred to gender. The pictures were all in black and white, so Gloria could only assume that the other letters were perhaps hair or eye colour. She fans them out on the bed, and removes the ones of Isabel. Like the other children, she was posed in a grotesquely sexual way. Most of the boys were shown naked; the girls sometimes wore booties, or vests. He had destroyed a duplicate set of photographs, in which all the children were fully clothed, before going to hospital. Every day he had chosen a different one to carry in his wallet.

Gloria chooses a photograph of Isabel – nine months old, naked, hips raised by a pillow, legs apart – and slips it into an envelope. She sweeps the surface of the drawer with her hand and finds one more photograph. Isabel's steady gaze meets hers. Eight years old. Standing with her back against a rough plaster wall. Gloria places it next to the other one, inside the envelope, and scoops the remaining photographs from the bed into the metal basket under the open window. Then adds a burning match, and watches the flames burn it all down to ashes.

Ruth calls from the kitchen and Gloria hurries out, closing the door behind her. In her hand she is holding a notepad, and a pen, as well as the envelope, now addressed to Isabel. She stuffs the envelope into the left pocket of her cardigan.

"Something burning in the kitchen?" Gloria asks as she passes Ruth on her way to the green chair in the sun on the balcony.

"No, I thought it came from your bedroom."

"Must be outside then, there have been fires all over. Bloody wind."

Gloria asks for a glass of water and walks to the chair. Ruth hears her mutter something, then a loud sigh follows. She gulps down the water. There is a rustling of paper.

Then silence.

Ruth allows her to sleep until the last minute, while she fills a plastic lunchbox with brightly coloured sweets to keep Gloria happy on the three-hour journey. *Padkos.* Fills a flask with coffee for her.

Then unpacks Gloria's kitchen cupboard and does a thorough cleaning.

She starts with the knives.

The woman in the white veil walks to the green chair where her daughter lies, fast asleep. She kneels next to the chair and strokes the wispy strands of hair on Gloria's head with one hand; with the other she traces the outline of the face of the young child in the photograph that lies on top of the envelope.

Isabel

"What a relief after the heat of last week," I say, backing out with the bucket of roses, bumping my head on the doorframe of the car. Morgan runs from the house, pulling on her raincoat, one hand holding an umbrella. She takes the flowers from me.

"All my favourite colours! Thanks Mom. Here, take the umbrella. I'll sort them out while you unpack. Did you bring some vases?"

"Damn, I forgot. Sorry!"

"It's okay, I'll make a plan."

I watch Morgan as she runs through the rain, back to the house. Frankie's genes were passed down to my daughter, re-assembled rather more successfully in a female form. As his familiar shape emerged during Morgan's adolescent years, I felt a tight emotion holding me back, forming a barrier between my daughter and me. It was hard to separate the memories of my grandfather from my daughter's familiar form, her body reminding me of him every day.

I wondered whether the genes determining the physical have emotional counterparts – I had in mind one of those cardboard wheels that turn over two rectangular windows, sometimes found in washing powder packs, presenting a stain – *blood* – in one window, with the solution – *bicarbonate of soda* – visible in the other window. When you turn it, another stain with its appropriate solvent opens. What if genes pre-determine everything? Turn the wheel to *high hips*, and the counterpart could be *deviousness*. *Short upper body* could indicate *sexual deviation*.

We run with bags of groceries between the car and the house until they are all inside. Morgan walks to the table and places a large stone in the centre of the table.

"You've been working hard!" I place a pack of white Sabbath candles on the kitchen counter. "The labyrinth is looking fantastic. And everything else, I haven't seen the house looking this festive in a long time."

"Ooh," she says, picking up the rope of fairy lights, "Just what I need."

"I'll make some tea." I say.

"Why don't you pour some wine? There's a cold white in the fridge. And an open red on the blue cupboard. Then come outside, we can sit on the *stoep*, or do you think we'll get too wet? I want to ask you something."

"Outside is fine, I love the rain." I sit down next to Morgan, and pass her a glass of wine. She gives me a piece of paper with the poem, *Bewys*, copied on it.

"Timo read this at your house the other day, and liked it. Have you translated it yet?"

"Close to finished with it. Do you want to hear it?"

"Please."

"Proof. A moment posed, created/you and me, arms encircled/the focus within/you in a shirt of blue cotton/your lemonskin intoxicating/I hold the proof of 3 x 5/of you and me and paradise."

I pass the poem back to her. "It's much more difficult translating a small poem with a big heart than a big one with a small heart. The heartbeat of a poem is conveyed by its rhythm, and if you lose that in the translation, the poem dies."

We continue to sit in silence. Morgan's glass of wine stands untouched on the low wall of the stoep. I wanted to have some time alone with her before everybody arrives, but can't find the right words to begin. She turns to me and says, "Let's play a

198

game for old times' sake; like we used to in the car driving to school . . . do you remember?"

"I remember you memorising your biology notes . . . you were completely obsessed."

"Well, I was. But what I want is one more guessing game."

"Of me telling you a story of some kind of natural, biological wonder and then you have to guess true . . . or false?"

"Exactly."

"Hmm, let me think . . . I think I know one that you haven't heard before. Are you ready?"

Morgan nods, and I start, using my dramatic story-telling voice. She moves a little closer.

"There is a wasp out there in the world, wherever it is that these wasps live, in a far-away jungle I suppose, with deep purple wings and orange legs."

"You're making it kind of obvious, Mom . . . "

"No, don't be so quick to judge, just listen. For its species to survive it needs to hijack a spider by injecting it with a paralysing poison, so that the spider can't move. The wasp then deposits a single egg into the spider's body while beating its purple wings excitedly; its orange legs dance a frenzy of malice."

A reluctant giggle escapes from Morgan's lips.

"After a few minutes, the spider wakes up, unaware that it now carries its own murderer deep inside its body. It feels a little confused, even dizzy, but puts it down to gorging on mosquitoes the previous night. If you have to give your answer now, what would it be? Fact, or fiction?"

"Oh Mom, I don't know! You make things up all the time . . . but it could be true . . . is it?"

"Wait till you hear the end, then make up your mind."

I turn to look at Morgan and say, "You look a lot like my grandfather, Frankie. Have I ever told you that?"

Morgan doesn't answer; her mind is with the growing baby-bud inside her. She opens her mouth to blurt it out, but finds her voice talking of Gloria.

"What is it that Gloria did to you that you can't forgive?"

I drain the last of my wine and get up from the bench. "Time to get ready," I say. "*Your* grandmother and Gloria are on their way, and, if I am not mistaken, more food."

The house is full of Morgan's succulents and her soft cushions and Timo's gentle sculptures. Morgan takes one of the soft purple velvet cushions from the couch and hugs it tightly against her stomach.

The roses are still in the bucket. They haven't travelled well, and are looking rather limp and droopy.

"Help me with this," Morgan says, and passes me a pair of kitchen scissors. On the draining board next to the sink is an assortment of twenty cups or so, without their saucers, leftovers from various sets. She takes out a yellow rose, Germiston Gold, and snips its stem three inches from the bud.

"Let's put them in the cups, threes or twos, they can stand on the stoepwall outside, welcoming everybody."

We stand side by side and cut the stems of the roses until they all rest inside the water-filled cups. We carry them outside.

"Beautiful," I say, and turn to Morgan. It feels important that we stay in this happy mood, and not spoil it with old arguments.

"Yes, it does look lovely," she says, hands on hips, admiring the row of roses. "But tell me, to get back to Gloria, what did she do to you?"

When I open my mouth to speak, my throat constricts, just like it did when Frankie pushed his tongue deep down into my mouth. I swallow hard and say: "You don't need to know, it is something I can't share with you, not yet, maybe never."

Morgan's face reflects the turmoil I feel inside. My daughter is crying. I haven't seen her cry since she was a child. Stonewall.

"Why won't you tell me? How can I bring a child into this family of secrets and whispers? I need to know!"

*

A week after Frankie's fifty-second birthday party, Ruth took me back to my grandparents' house, ignoring all my protestations. I didn't know how I could ever look at my grandmother again, the memory of the dark blur of her nipples spreading like a stain behind my eyelids. Ruth got into the car, and we drove there in silence. My grandfather was at the gate to meet us, telling Ruth not to worry.

"She seems scared of Gloria . . . how is she today?"

My mother placed my hand in my grandfather's.

"Oh," Frankie replied, "You know what it's like, Ruth. Your mother is not strong. She's still sleeping, but I'll look after Isabel, nothing to worry about."

My hand grew clammy in his grip, which tightened as I tried to slip free. As soon as the car disappeared around the corner, he dropped to his haunches, the fabric of his pants straining across his thighs. He looked me straight in the eyes, and said, "So, here's my little thief, the little snoop. Who would ever have thought our innocent little Isabel had it in her?"

My throat tightened and squeezed the life from any words I might have spoken, as if still trying to swallow that sharp-edged photograph. I couldn't look at him. His hand gripped my shoulder as he pushed himself upright.

"First, a photograph."

He smoothed my hair down, then rubbed with his thumb across my mouth.

"Then I'll teach you a lesson you bloody well won't forget, my girl!" he shouted over his shoulder as he walked to the house to fetch his camera. I stood with my back against the warm wall, waiting for him to return.

Gloria's face appeared in the window as he pulled me towards the ivy-covered wall of their back garden. She held the curtain to one side and watched through tendrils of smoke, sucking hard on a cigarette.

His rough hands fumbled with my dress, and then pulled a limp bit of flesh from his trousers. It reminded me of the unbaked bread rolls lined up on a greased tray in my mother's kitchen. He held it in one hand while forcing the other into my panties. I wept and gagged on his tongue, pushing down my throat, and felt a hot stream of urine running down my legs. For two years, until he died, I endured this monthly ritual.

The shame of it burnt like a hot knife, slashing.

That same feeling now closes my throat to the words my daughter wants to hear. I will not tell her.

"No. Not all secrets need to be revealed. This has nothing to do with you."

I grab her arm, spilling wine. "What! What did you say just now? About bringing a child into this family?"

Ruth

Freshly baked bread and the warm breastmilk excreta of small babies share the same smell. Yeasty. On the back seat of the car, next to Gloria, the two loaves of bread steam, wrapped in fresh dishcloths – their smell mingling with that of stale urine. Ruth had baked the loaves, even though Isabel asked her not to.

"No Mom, I'll get everything, just relax and be there," her daughter instructed.

This means that she will have to sneak the loaves into the house past Isabel's thin-lipped disapproval and give them to Morgan, who loves Ruth's home-baked food; never looks a gift horse in the mouth.

The landscape blurs by, dulled by familiarity, and obscured by a steady downpour of rain that has appeared, seemingly from nowhere. From the back, she hears Gloria's dry snores, as her mother drifts in and out of sleep.

Ruth approaches the narrow pass just before the hairpin bend outside Villiersdorp. She adjusts her rear-view mirror, to catch a glimpse of Gloria.

"Is your old house in Worcester still standing?"

Ruth glances over her shoulder towards Gloria, who is struggling upright, unsnapping the safety belt. She opens her handbag and takes out the Tupperware container filled with sweets, offering some to Ruth.

"No thanks . . . damn . . . we're stuck . . . just look at these bloody trucks!"

Ruth meets up with a large farm truck, fully laden with

wooden crates. In the rear-view mirror she notices another approaching from behind.

"Damn, this is all I need now!"

She slaps the steering wheel with the heel of her hand, slips the gear-stick into first, and changes the setting of the windscreen wipers. Their frantic pace increases her sense of panic. Loud sucking noises from the back seat fill the air, releasing a sweet smell, which, added to the faint urine smell already present, causes red prickles of irritation to surface on Ruth's chest.

She opens her window and adjusts her side mirror, as if this might make the trucks disappear. A blast of rain blows into the car. Firmly wedged between the trucks she crawls up the steep hairpin bend.

"What are you doing, Ma? Stop it!"

Ruth scowls at the mirror, trying to see why Gloria is kicking the back of her seat like a naughty two-year old. She reaches with her left hand between the seats to the back and gives Gloria's knee a little shake.

"What's going on . . . what are you doing?"

Her mother's hand grips hers, squeezes it hard, trying to pull Ruth towards her. The car skids to the left and Ruth grabs the steering wheel with both hands to steer it through its free-floating swerve. The wipers continue their frantic movement across the window, sweeping away sheets of water. Ruth glances back and sees her mother's purple face, hands clutched around her throat. Her eyes are wide open, streaming tears of agony. Choking, wheezing sounds fill the car. The two truck drivers misunderstand the loud hooting from Ruth's car, and gesture their response.

She is wedged tight with no room to move over.

An eternity later she reaches the top of the road where she pulls into the lookout point clearing. The car stalls to a shuddering halt as she half-falls out, struggling with her seatbelt, and finally pulls Gloria from the back and onto the wet gravel. Her mother remains limp and lifeless as Ruth repeats, for the last time, the familiar routine of searching her mother's throat with her index finger.

Words explode, small incoherent sounds, as she finds the obstruction and slides the sticky sweet from Gloria's mouth. She picks up the lifeless body and eases it onto the back seat of the car. Then smoothes down Gloria's dress, soaked-through and muddy. She wipes her mother's mouth, too roughly, with numbed hands. Her hand knocks against Gloria's teeth. Backing out of the car, she sees an envelope lying on the wet ground. Raindrops have streaked Isabel's name. Ruth opens the envelope and takes out two photographs. The top one shows Isabel posed against Frankie's garage wall. She turns it over, and reveals the second one.

"Oh *God*, no, no, no," she whimpers, walking blindly through the rain, away from the car, away from Gloria. Her eyes are locked onto the halo of Isabel's curls, her thumb covering her baby's body. She stops, and takes the letter from the envelope. Reads the few lines scattered like broken spider legs across the page – Gloria's plea for forgiveness.

The heels of her shoes sink deep into the mud, rooting her. Returning both photographs and the letter to the envelope, she frees her feet and takes her cellphone from her pocket, then dials a number. When she turns around she stumbles to her knees. The envelope blows from her hand as she grabs at a grassy shrub growing on the edge of the cliff. Its roots tear free from the rain-soaked soil.

Her fall is soundless.

*

Half an hour later a small green Golf arrives. Jonathan and Timo get out. Ruth is nowhere to be seen. Looking up, Timo spots her navy shoes in the distance, near the lookout point. He rushes towards the edge, and peers over. Running back to the car he bends down to pick up an envelope addressed to Isabel.

Gloria lies, a bundle of rags on the back seat, next to two loaves of bread.

It has stopped raining.

Gloria

Dear Isabel

Soft sap rising through the wetness –
They all scuttle about chasing their tails trying to figure me
out. Meaningless. Escape into a bottle of winged seeds that rests
among underwear in a forgotten drawer. A dress for Ruth, which
she never wore. Words tumble into my head like frogs after the
rain. I have to put my knitting aside for a moment, all that
wrinkled, dry skin!

I pulled lace across a window, once, but still I saw it all. Dear
Isabel – what big eyes you had! You will never have those curls
again. Once you cut them, they are gone forever.

Soft sap rising budlets purpling –
a yellow-tinged curve. I am a downward ripple into darkness.

Forgive me,
Your grandmother Gloria.

Isabel

The phone rings. Morgan gets up to answer it. As she walks to the phone I imagine the hill of belly still to come. My child, a mother.

"Hello, Morgan Stone?"

She always answers the phone that way, as if questioning her own identity. "It's Dad," she mouths to me.

Then her face crumples. I get up and stand next to her, waiting. She nods her head. She holds out the receiver, hugs me, sobbing.

Their arrival looks like the opening scene of a horror film. The sun is about to set and its last rays paint a backdrop of vermilion; red raindrops slide from leaves and branches. The flashing light on top of the ambulance roof churns into the pools of water lying on the ground. Timo's green car follows.

I walk past Morgan and down the steps of the stoep. Jonathan and Timo are getting out of the car. Timo walks to Morgan and hands her two loaves of bread, wrapped in my mother's favourite faded blue dishcloth. I walk towards Jonathan, who opens his arms to receive me. He carefully pulls a soggy letter from his shirt pocket.

"Timo found this, close to where she . . . went over. I still can't believe it – this must give some clue to what happened. She probably meant to give it you tonight."

I recognise my grandmother's handwriting, streaked with rain. Inside, I find two photographs. One is of a child posed against a grainy plaster wall. It is the photograph Frankie took that day; minutes after Ruth and David had sped away in their car to the farm.

Bewys.

With the impotent sense of abandonment that only children feel, I had looked over my grandfather's shoulder as the car turned the corner and disappeared from sight. As he clicked the shutter, I heard him say: "I want to take a picture, proof that you are my prettiest little girl."

I close my eyes and see the ivy tumble over a wall, a waterfall of green stars. Once again, I feel the pointy leaves prick my back. My grandfather pushes me deeper into the hedge until I disappear into the undergrowth, a lace-winged insect, now shredded and torn. The edge of a leaf, serrated like Ruth's carving knife, shifts into focus. All the words that Frankie made me swallow now rise in a wave of panic.

I read my grandmother's letter, folded around the second photograph. Looking at it I see, once more, the flash of my grandfather's camera, his winking eye. I drop the envelope and turn blindly, feeling Morgan's fingers brush against my arm. The cow's low mooing follows me as I walk into the mouth of the labyrinth. I begin to run, spiralling to the centre, and the world spins away from me until only sky remains. At the heart of the labyrinth I lie down, leaning my back against the stonewall. Morgan crouches next to me.

"I don't understand," she says.

I am lying with my cheek against the ground, and notice a row of ants move past. I imagine my mother with me and say to her, "Ants *don't* crawl, you know." I watch as they disappear into a hole in the ground, carrying bits of food. I press my cheek closer, closer to the child trapped in the reflection of my mother's polished kitchen floor.

My heartbeat is strong and steady, its rhythm rooting me to the ground.

One long month has passed since the funeral. I have begun to unravel the dresses Gloria knitted over the years, most in tomato-coloured lambswool. I washed them – not thinking that the wool might shrink – but the knots have shrunk tight into themselves, resisting my efforts.

But I persist. I need to unravel, to undo. To find the knots, the knobbly bits, and the dropped stitches. Not that Gloria was likely to drop many stitches – an accomplished knitter, she chose, always, the difficult patterns. Dresses that no one ever wore.

A beep from my cellphone announces a message from Morgan. *Found veggie haggis in Edinburgh! Yum!*

Sitting cross-legged on the carpet in my bedroom, I can smell my mother's kitchen, see the row of knives against the wall. "A blunt knife is more dangerous," Ruth often told me, and kept her knives safely sharp. Small cuts on the pad of her thumb, tiny nicks on the tips of her fingers, oven element burns – her hands scarred from feeding her family.

She had come from a long line of kitchen warriors.

Her death was accidental. That, at least, is the official version, the one that most people choose to believe. They cling to the uprooted shrub as irrefutable proof.

But I know the truth.

I cut the first knot, and the tension releases, allowing row after row of stitches to unravel effortlessly. I will knit a red blanket for my grandson, to keep him warm in Scotland.

The unravelling becomes a meditation.

I come to another knot, and see my grandmother's hand reaching into her basket. She picks up a ball of wool to tie onto the short strand left from the previous one. Gloria's hands had held these same strands of wool almost seventy years ago.

In the margins of her knitting patterns I discovered scribbled alterations. She never liked instructions – being told what to do.

Among the scribbles are some enigmatic bits, like *Remember to forget*. Now, these words resemble the calm surface of the sea after the southeaster has blown for a week or more, as waves gently break below the surface.

Some days after the funeral, while Morgan and I were walking on the beach together, she asked for the ending of the wasp story.

"The purple wasp with the orange legs? I forgot where I got to . . . "

"I think up to where the wasp stings the spider and lays the eggs in its body?"

"Okay . . . I remember . . . well, the spider lurches away, carrying its own murderer inside its body. For once, predator becomes prey. The larvae hatch a few days later, and start sucking the blood of the spider. Eventually they take over the spider's brain, and reprogramme it to spin a web of strong cables. These are useless to a spider, of course, but perfect for the wasps to hang cocoons from. Afterwards, the spider moves to the middle of the web, and slowly starves to death."

"Is that it?" she asked, hooking her arm through mine, "End of spider?"

"Hmm . . . not quite . . . the hatched larvae then feast on the spider until they are sated. Then start to spin their own cocoons."

We had reached the wall on the south side of the beach, and turned around.

"*Now* tell me," I said, "Fact, or fiction?"